The Leftover Kid

Joanne Stanbridge

June, 2000

*Congratulations,
Kristyn
on participating in the
Red Cedar Awards!*

Mrs. Johnson

NORTHERN LIGHTS YOUNG NOVELS

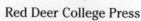

Red Deer College Press

About the Author

JOANNE STANBRIDGE holds a Masters Degree in Creative Writing from Concordia University, and she has published poetry, library-related articles and book reviews. *The Leftover Kid* is her first novel, which she says started out as an assignment on the poet Emily Dickenson. "Unfortunately," she says, "'Dickenson' falls close to 'Dionne Quintuplets' in the encyclopedia, and it only took a few seconds for me to get hooked on this amazing episode in Canadian history."

Northern Lights Young Novels are published by
Red Deer College Press
56 Avenue & 32 Street
Red Deer Alberta Canada T4N 5H5

Acknowledgments
Edited for the Press by Peter Carver
Cover art and design by Jeffrey Hitch
Text design by Dennis Johnson
Printed and Bound in Canada by Webcom Limited for Red Deer College Press

Financial support provided by the Alberta Foundation for the Arts, a beneficiary of the Lottery Fund of the Government of Alberta, and by the Canada Council, the Department of Canadian Heritage, and Red Deer College.

THE CANADA COUNCIL | LE CONSEIL DES ARTS
FOR THE ARTS | DU CANADA
SINCE 1957 | DEPUIS 1957

COMMITTED TO THE DEVELOPMENT OF CULTURE AND THE ARTS

Canadian Cataloguing in Publication Data
Stanbridge, Joanne, 1960–
The leftover kid

(Northern lights young novels)
ISBN 0-88995-160-8

I. Title. II. Series.
PS8587.T29L43 1997   jC813'.54   C96-910776-5
PZ7.S78617Le 1997

6 5 4 3 2 1

Author's Acknowledgments

I owe special thanks to Tim Wynne-Jones, whose expert guidance kept this vessel on course; to Peter Carver, who gallantly took the oars mid-stream; to friends and family, who supplied life rafts and safety lines, and to the residents of Podwater Mansion—especially Dian—who stocked the galley with scones and rice pudding to see me through the voyage. Thank you so much!

–JS

For Katherine Judith Alexander,
who asked, "What do you really want?"
until I came to my senses

Chapter 1

I became famous last year, when my mother married the prime minister of Canada.

Before the wedding, I used to be a normal girl, living in a regular apartment and going to an ordinary school. But then my mother met Jordan Sweetwine, and they fell in love. The next thing I knew, my mother was on the news, slipping her hand into the crook of the prime minister's arm and smiling up at him while they announced their engagement. It was a smile I'd never seen before. It made her look all soft and hopeful, like a stranger on one of those sappy commercials that make you feel like crying. While Mr. Sweetwine smiled back at her, and their interviewer beamed delightedly, I sat on the shaggy carpet in front of our TV, throwing potato chips at the screen and sobbing.

Everybody wanted to talk about the wedding. My teachers congratulated me and smiled and asked about it. The other kids gaped at me or pestered me with questions. Mrs. Glickman, in apartment 1408, cornered me near the mailboxes and wanted to know what I thought of Mr. Sweetwine and my future stepsisters, and whether my mother would quit her job as a psychologist, and how I felt about moving into the prime minister's official residence.

I hated that. Everyone wanted to know about the Sweetwines. How could I tell them I had never met my family-to-be? My mother tried again and again to introduce me to Mr. Sweetwine, but every meeting was postponed or cancelled. The international trade negotiations broke down. Mr. Sweetwine had to fix them. The president of a foreign nation died. Mr. Sweetwine had to go to the funeral. The U.S. president called an emergency meeting. Mr. Sweetwine scribbled me an apology as he hurried to catch his plane, and when my mother handed it to me, her face was sorrowful.

You're probably not surprised to hear that the president of the United States is more important than an eleven-year-old future stepdaughter. But I don't mind telling you that my feelings were hurt. As I watched the two men shake hands on the news that night, my mother hugged me and kissed the top of my head, and said, *"Stop* throwing pretzels at the TV !"

She wanted me to meet the prime minister's daughters. I didn't want to. She thought I should phone them. I said, "No." Then she put her foot down and said I should at least write them a letter, which I did. I wrote three pages. My mother read the letter and said she'd lie down and die before she delivered such a thing, and what did I have against those five adorable girls anyway?

I didn't have anything personal against them. I had never met them. But you could hardly open a magazine or turn on the TV without seeing the latest photos of the nation's darlings, the Sweetwine quintuplets, the five identical miracle children whose father was the prime minister of the country and whose mother had died when they were only a few weeks old. The quintuplets were beautiful and charming and famous. Their life was much bigger than mine. I did not know how to be their sister.

"They act like babies," I protested.

My mother frowned. Then she pursed her lips and nodded. "Maybe you're right. They've led a very sheltered life. Maybe they have been encouraged to stay more sweet and innocent than other eleven-year-olds."

I rolled my eyes.

"But maybe you can be a good influence on them," she said. "Did you ever think of that?"

I didn't want to be an influence. I didn't want anything to do with them. And the more my mother pushed me, the more wild and stubborn I felt, until one day she sighed angrily and shoved the hair back from her forehead and said, "All right. You win. I won't say another word about it. You and the quintuplets will just have to work it out after the wedding."

Which made it sound as if they had been complaining about me. I had not expected that. It made me furious. Also, I started to get scared. As the wedding drew closer, it was like being in a giant bathtub, getting sucked closer and closer to the drain hole, spinning toward the dark and horrible unknown.

You probably remember the ceremony, which took place at the end of April. I'm sure you saw it on television.

I jammed myself into the vestibule of the church with the radiant bride and a couple of bodyguards, some hairdressers and wedding consultants and, of course, the Sweetwine quintuplets. Everyone talked in frantic whispers, giggling and saying, "Shh!" and bumping into one another, but the quintuplets did not speak to me and I made sure not to look at any of them. My taffeta dress rustled like tissue paper. The wreath of flowers made my forehead itch, and my hands were slippery on my bouquet.

Big wooden doors blocked our view into the church, but the stained glass windows above them shone weirdly, lit up by television lights. Behind me, a woman murmured into a microphone: "The six girls line up . . . the Sweetwine quintuplets first: Lianne, then Suzanne, followed by Anne, Diane, and Marianne. Our viewers at home will notice that each girl's initial has been beautifully embroidered on her sash. It is quite a shock to see these five. They are absolutely identical. And don't they look gorgeous?"

The reporter let out a little sigh of delight before she continued, ". . . the bride's daughter, Willa Killick-Whimsey, will bring up the rear . . . this must be one of the most unique bridal parties in Canadian history."

A tall thin man with a gold earring shushed us and herded us into position.

". . . These five little darlings," whispered the reporter, "are delighted to welcome Louise Killick as their lovely new step-mother."

The music ballooned out, making the stone church vibrate. The doors opened and the first quintuplet stepped into the glare. Instantly, there was a thundering sound, like a great wave, as hundreds of spectators heaved themselves to their feet. I tried not to look at them. I stared instead at the red carpet, which stretched endlessly toward the altar, toward Mr. Sweetwine, who stood beaming in his black tuxedo. No national emergency had prevented him from showing up at his wedding. There he was, in real life.

Bodyguards slid like shadows along the edges of the procession. The second quintuplet stepped onto the red carpet and then the third.

A murmur of delight and approval went up from the congregation and filled the church. It hovered in the rafters.

The fourth quintuplet, then the fifth, began to move down the aisle. Everywhere I looked, people's eyes were wide with wonder and excitement. Those sleek quintuplet heads and perfect dresses stretched in a tidy line that seemed to link me with the faraway prime minister.

I stepped into the aisle.

I suppose it did look funny. If you had seen five identical girls come through a doorway, followed by another girl who was completely different, you might laugh, too.

But it surprised me. The mutter of admiration broke up into a chuckling river of laughter that swept from the back of the church to the front, running through the pews and around the pillars and into the shadowy corners.

All I could see were hundreds of mouths full of teeth, eyes crinkled up with amusement, and too-bright lights. I stopped.

My mother nearly bumped into me.

I've seen the pictures. I know my freckles were standing out like splotches. I know my rumpled hair made me look like a squirrel. I know I forgot to smile, even though my mother and the wedding planners and the man with the gold earring had reminded me a hundred times.

People were whispering.

My mother reached around her huge bouquet and put her hand on my shoulder.

"It's all right," she said. "Go."

I went.

At the front of the church, while my mother and Mr. Sweetwine said their vows, I stood very still. When everyone sang, I listened. When everyone prayed, I looked at my shiny black shoes. When I was supposed to sit, I sat, and when it was time to stand, I stood.

The ceremony took a long time. When it was over, I followed

the happy couple along the red carpet. I kept my chin up and my eyes fixed on the vestibule.

That's when it happened. My mother reached out to kiss someone, pausing for one brief second. I stepped on the hem of her dress, the sole of my new shoe slid across the satin as if it were sheer ice, and I fell.

The five girls behind me kept going. They piled into me like a bunch of penguins, and down we all tumbled onto the red carpet—one glorious tangle of taffeta and patent leather and petals and beautifully embroidered sashes.

"Oh!" cried a man on my left.

"Oh!" shouted everyone else, shoving into the aisle. My mother and Mr. Sweetwine whirled toward us, their shocked faces looming. Worried adults pushed from all sides, demanding, "Are you all right? Are you all right?" and reaching out to untangle us. Our floral wreaths were crooked or missing, and our bouquets were crushed. The carpet was littered with petals and bits of fern. Camera operators clambered onto the pews to get a better view.

The quintuplet under my left elbow was Marianne—her sash with its embroidered "M" dangled across my knee. For a second, I thought she was going to cry. But when I glanced back at the fallen quintuplets, with their red faces and their messed-up hair, the whole thing seemed suddenly ridiculous, and a howl of crazy laughter bubbled up inside me. I clamped my lips around it and struggled to remain solemn, but Marianne saw it and stared.

"Willa!" my mother cried, reaching down to haul me to my feet. "What happened? Are you okay?"

"I'm sorry," I said. "I slipped."

I was trying so hard to be serious that the last word squeaked, and then the laughter just burst out of me, surprising my mother and making Mr. Sweetwine blink.

"I can't help it," I gasped.

"Stop it this instant," whispered my mother, as she dusted me off and pushed the bouquet back into my hands.

"But they went down like bowling pins," I protested, and that set me off again. Behind me, the quintuplets were on their feet again while dozens of people helped them straighten their dresses and tidy their hair.

But something else was happening. Marianne had begun to grin as if my laughter had infected her. I peeked up at Mr. Sweetwine, whose mouth was grave, and discovered a glint of humor in his eye. Around us, people had begun to chuckle, and as we straggled toward the vestibule, I heard more than one quintuplet giggling.

As my new stepsisters passed down the aisle, dozens of cameras clicked and whirred. Reporters ran, crouched, and leaned from the choir loft.

I led the string of identical darlings back out through the wooden doors and stopped, turning to share one more snort of embarrassed laughter with them, but they were already gone. Bodyguards shepherded them through a side exit, down the stone steps, and into a limousine waiting at the curb.

My mother kissed me. A whiff of her perfume twined around me as she gave me an extra hug, full of happiness and excitement.

"Are you all right?" she whispered. "These things happen. Don't worry about it."

But a big woman in a gray coat was shoving from behind, and a blonde woman squealed and grabbed at my mother, and people were reaching for Mr. Sweetwine, who began to shake hands with everyone in sight.

The man with the gold earring pulled at my sleeve and swept me into a cloakroom, where I sat down on a little bench. I wasn't laughing anymore. There was a carpet burn on my wrist and my legs were shaking.

"The limousine will take you to your father's apartment in Montreal," he said. "Wait here."

Just around the corner, a reporter was saying, ". . . And so, after twelve years in office, Jordan Sweetwine begins another chapter of his extraordinary life. As he heads into this election year his popularity has never been higher . . . and his much-loved family continues to capture hearts here in Canada and around the globe."

As you probably know, the Sweetwine quintuplets are the most famous children in the world. And I think you'd have to agree that their father is *practically* as famous as they are.

Well, now my mother is married to him.

Chapter 2

I went to stay with my father for a month while my mother and Mr. Sweetwine were on their honeymoon. It was a quiet time, just working with Dad in the flower shop or drinking tea with him in the evenings. He didn't talk much about my mother, but now and then she would appear on the news—fuzzy and gray and hard to see on my father's little black-and-white TV—and Dad would stop what he was doing to squint at the screen as if he were puzzling over something. If I'd known what he was thinking, I might have paid more attention.

But I had problems of my own. Before long, it was time for me to move into the prime minister's official residence.

My first glimpse of the Sweetwine quintuplets after the frenzied half-hour of the wedding was not exactly reassuring. To get to them, I passed through the security gate, the main entrance flanked by uniformed Mounties, the vestibule, the foyer, and the lower entryway only to find that my mother and Mr. Sweetwine had been delayed en route from Hong Kong. There was no familiar face to greet me.

I found the quintuplets posed on the grand staircase in the upper entryway, having their picture taken. I can't tell you what a jolt it gives you to see those five identical faces watching you with undisguised curiosity. When you first see them, you feel the surprise in the middle of your stomach. You study one quint's face. Then you look at the girl beside her and find exactly the same face blinking at you. So you focus on *that* face, only to look at another and receive the same shock again. Your eyes start jumping from quint to quint as you struggle to find one tiny difference that will let you tell them apart. Meanwhile, they sit opening and closing their eyes like five wise owls.

I summoned all my courage and addressed my new family for the first time.

"Where's my mother?"

No one moved. The five National Treasures on the stairs were dressed in stiff plaid jumpers, neat blouses, and saddle shoes. I felt this made an interesting contrast to my denim and silver skirt, yellow runners, and hot-pink sweatshirt with the words *I don't get MAD, I get EVEN* in big letters.

While Nanny Grayson, the quints' governess, stood gaping, the photographer snapped a picture of me.

"Stop that," I said.

Nanny Grayson found her voice. "Yes, stop it, Gordon. You idiot."

The five on the stairs exploded into giggles, and somebody behind the dining-room door smothered a gasp. I found out later this was Mrs. Gummidge, the cook, who happened to glance through a crack in the door at the moment of my arrival.

The photographer tried to settle his jangled nerves by taking another picture. The flash seemed to restore Nanny Grayson's legendary unflappability. She snatched the camera from him, fired a quelling look at the quintuplets, and blinked at me.

"Willa," she said, "there must be some mistake. We phoned your father's shop in Montreal to tell him your mother's plane was delayed. You weren't supposed to arrive for another five hours."

"But the limousine showed up at ten-thirty," I protested, "and Dad said I should come after all. He said everything must have gotten sorted out." It hurt to say his name. I swallowed hard. "I didn't even get to see the end of *Canada This Week.*"

There was a long pause.

"Well," said Nanny Grayson at last, "it's just a little mix-up, that's all. We're glad you're here."

Silence. They didn't *seem* glad. Those identical gazes fixed on me like the eyes of five peregrine falcons. I stood examining the black and white floor tiles, which stretched out in every direction.

"Ladies?" she prompted.

14

"Hello," murmured the quintuplets. The photographer strangled a laugh, but Nanny Grayson shoved the camera into his hands and directed him firmly toward the door. "Official photos of the arrival are tomorrow at noon. See you then, Gordon. Thanks so much. Bye, now."

Before he could stammer out a single question, she had steered him down the steps into the lower entryway and around the corner. She was slim and young and pretty, and she smiled so charmingly as she threw him out that he did not try very hard to resist. She came back with her hands on her hips.

"Well, then. Shall we go up and get acquainted?"

I was exhausted and desperate. I'd packed the *Happy Dooley* books in my suitcase, and I was longing to lose myself in the comfortable look and smell of those familiar pages, but something had been preying on me during the whole limousine ride and I wanted to get it off my chest right away.

"My mother promised I could have my own room."

I don't know what they were expecting me to say, but this was clearly not it. Nanny Grayson's eyebrows crept up her forehead.

"You don't want to join the quints in their room?"

"No." I said it firmly.

"You're sure?"

Maybe they hadn't fixed a separate place for me. Maybe there wasn't any room in this house for someone who couldn't be a sixth quintuplet. Maybe they expected me to dissolve myself into their perfectly arranged, prepackaged, nationally televised lives.

"I'm sure," I said through clenched teeth.

"We'll show you upstairs, then," said Nanny Grayson. "Come on, ladies."

The room they gave me was cool, blue, and quiet.

The quints skittered around in the doorway, peeking at me, while Nanny Grayson showed me how to work all the light switches and the window blinds. She showed me the closet. When she showed me how to open and close the drawers, I knew she was killing time, waiting for me to unpack my suitcase, to get friendly with the quints, and to start asking sprightly questions about the official residence.

I pulled a *Maclean's* magazine from the outside pocket of my suitcase, settled myself cross-legged on the bed, and began to read.

She raised her eyebrows at the magazine, studied the top of my head for a long moment, and said, "Would you like to choose a more . . . suitable . . . book from the girls' room?"

"No," I said.

She wrinkled up her forehead, watched me for a minute more, and went out, shooing the quints ahead of her.

When I was sure she wasn't coming back, I got up and closed the door. I wasn't really in the mood for *Maclean's,* but to tell you the truth, I don't like anyone to see me reading *The Happy Dooleys on Location.*

I don't know if you're familiar with the *Happy Dooley* books. They were written a long time ago, when my mother was a child. When I found them at the library book sale, she took one look and told me to put them back. She said they were outdated. She said they were trashy. She said they were full of *very* poor role models.

There were two *Dooley* books in the book sale. When my mother wasn't looking, I bought them for fifty cents. They are thick and solid, with old stained pages as soft as flannel and the words *Discarded by Ottawa Public Library* stamped inside them. When I was younger, living in the apartment with my mother, I used to hide in my room and read *More Adventures of the Happy Dooleys* over and over. I almost thought I was Lucinda Dooley, who was eight years old in that book and lived in a big old house with her four sisters and three brothers, helping her mother in the kitchen while they waited for Mr. Dooley to come home from his job at the hardware store.

But for some reason these days I only wanted to read *The Happy Dooleys on Location.* I read it again and again. I read it so often I practically memorized it. When I climbed into bed at night, I dreamed I was the twelve-year-old Lucinda, sitting prettily in the department store window, modelling a velvet dress until a talent scout discovered her. I knew exactly how the other Dooleys reacted when my movie offer came and how it felt when we all moved to Hollywood and what it was like at the movie studio, where I charmed the aging actress and helped the leading man find his lost sweetheart, and how homesick we all became and how we returned at last to our big old house in Middleville, Illinois.

I knew things about the Happy Dooleys that weren't even written down in the books.

But I read them only when my door was firmly shut. When I lived in the apartment with my mother, I kept them on the top shelf of my closet, under a vaporizer and an old tennis racket.

That day—my first day at the official residence—I tried to read the last chapter, where the Dooleys finally arrive home and put the kettle on and take the dust sheets off the furniture and light a fire in the fireplace. But my eyes kept skipping and jumping over the words.

I could hear the Sweetwine quintuplets laughing and chattering in the playroom across the hall. They had not spoken a single word to me.

🍁 🍁 🍁

When Prime Minister Sweetwine and his lovely bride (my mother) arrived home from Hong Kong at five-thirty, I was still in my room. Later, Mrs. Gummidge filled me in on the details.

First, after the hugging and kissing was over, the radiant bride said, "Could you put that on the hall table, please?" and a servant carried in the largest bouquet of flowers Mrs. Gummidge had ever seen. (She just happened to be at the dining room door again. So was Wilton Amaryllis, the gardener, who grumbled, "Some crazy guy dropped that thing off at the gate. Security went over it petal by petal. Took the whole afternoon.")

Mrs. Gummidge says she didn't know the names of all the flowers in that gigantic bouquet—red ones the size of your hand, nodding blue ones, armfuls of pink and yellow rosebuds, and bursts of white, set in masses of fern. She says it just wasn't enough to call it a bouquet—it was a work of art.

"The card, ma'am," said the servant who carried the flowers.

"Oh, Jordan, you shouldn't have," said the blushing bride.

"I didn't. Ha-ha," said Mr. Sweetwine. "Read the card, darling. Solve the mystery for us."

My mother opened the envelope with a newly manicured fingernail and read the card silently. Her face crumpled. She read it again.

"Darling?" prompted Mr. Sweetwine.

"How nice," said my mother in a faint voice. "It's from

17

Howard . . . Willa's father. Congratulating us on the marriage."

"Well. Splendid," said Mr. Sweetwine.

My mother pressed the card to her heart. Mrs. Gummidge says you could see the poor woman's hand trembling, even from the dining room, as she said, "I guess I'm a little tired from all that travelling. I'll just unpack a few things before Willa arrives."

The quintuplets, who had been twittering around during the big arrival, couldn't restrain themselves. They cried out, "She's here already! . . . She's upstairs! . . . Everything got mixed up!"

My mother looked at Nanny Grayson, who said, "Yes, ma'am. A slight mix-up due to the delay in your flight. She's settling into her room right now."

You could call this an understatement. Nanny Grayson had tried to get me to come out three times, and each time she poked her head around the door I had tucked the *Happy Dooley* book under the pillow, snatched up *Maclean's,* and scowled fiercely. I had no intention of leaving my room without someone to protect me from those five pairs of laughing eyes.

"Well, if I could just see her . . ." said my mother.

I guess that's when I came out. The door slammed behind me, and the suitcase bumped from step to step as I stomped down the stairs, buttoning my coat with my free hand. All those eyes looked up. Inside, I was a tornado, whirling and furious.

"Sweetheart," gasped my mother.

"I hate this place," I said. "I'd rather go live with Dad."

For several seconds, no one spoke. Mr. Sweetwine's smile dimmed a few watts.

"Oh," said my mother in a broken voice. "Sweetheart."

I stood my ground. I glared. "You didn't come up to my room."

"Darling . . . I've only been home five minutes. I didn't even know you were here."

I stamped my foot.

"Well, why *didn't* you?" I yelled—and burst into tears.

My mother's eyes filled, too, as she ran forward to take me in her arms.

I stamped my foot again, buried my face in the good familiar smell of her neck, and howled. As she patted me anxiously and shrugged out of her pink silk jacket—first one arm and then the other—my father's card fell onto the black and white tiles. She didn't even notice it.

"We'll go upstairs," she said.

"Yes, upstairs," echoed Nanny Grayson.

"Upstairs," echoed quintuplet voices.

While the whole flurry of us started up the steps, Mr. Sweetwine scooped my mother's jacket from the floor. That's when it happened. The card tumbled free of the pink silk, slipped, and skittered across the tiles. It came to rest, face up, against the leg of the hall table.

Mr. Sweetwine read it. Everyone read it. Even I read it, later that evening, when I found it lying on the table.

LOUISE!
PLEASE COME BACK TO ME! I LOVE YOU!
HOWARD XOXOXOXO

And that's how all the trouble began.

Chapter 3

If you have ever lived in the official residence of the prime minister of Canada, you will remember the cook's sitting room, which is sandwiched between the kitchen and the upper entryway with its grand spiral staircase. A heavy door separates this part of the staff wing from the main house, and the family is never supposed to pass through it.

Unfortunately, no one had bothered to mention this to me, and the day after my arrival I showed up on Mrs. Gummidge's threshold. The expression on her face was somewhat less than welcoming.

"They want to take pictures," I said. "I have to get away."

She turned her face longingly toward the rerun of *Coronation Street* she'd been trying to watch. "They'll expect you to be in the photos."

"Yes."

That seemed to be the end of that conversation, so I tried another subject. "Is this the only TV in this whole house? How do they keep up with the news around here?"

"Mr. Sweetwine takes *three* newspapers," she informed me in frosty tones. "He's *very* familiar with the news."

I studied the row of African violets on the windowsill and frowned at the lawn beyond them, where the rain was streaming down.

"Now, I expect you're a bit homesick," she ventured after a moment. "It's perfectly natural."

"No," I said.

Mrs. Gummidge raised her eyebrows.

"I don't miss my mother's apartment," I said, "but I can't stop thinking about my father's flower shop. These violets smell just like it."

She knew what I meant. My parents had owned the flower shop until they got divorced three years ago, but my father still ran the shop and lived in the flat upstairs. You may have heard how I stayed with him for that month while my mother was on her honeymoon.

"Anyway," I said, "the thing is, they don't want me to wear this for the photo session."

She looked me over, from my yellow *Make My Day* sweatshirt and *Stop Acid Rain* button, down to my jeans and red hightop running shoes.

"They're expecting me to dress like the quints. For the photos. To show I'm part of the family and all."

My hands started shaking again, and I had to swallow hard. I wanted to say, "Not that I care," but I knew my voice would wobble, so I concentrated hard on the African violets. Finally, I said, "Of course, I could always go live with my dad."

She lifted an eyebrow. "You haven't been here long."

"No."

"It's bound to take a while to get used to us."

"I know."

She settled deeper into her chair and concentrated hard on the TV. Then she said, "I don't suppose they'd let you go back, even if you wanted to."

"No."

Behind me, the television made a murmuring sound. Mrs. Gummidge sniffed and adjusted one of the cushions, settling it more firmly behind her. "This evening," said the announcer, "on the six o'clock news. Is the honeymoon over? Just one month after the wedding, Louise Killick-Sweetwine receives a love letter from her ex-husband. Will there be trouble at 24 Sussex Drive? Stay tuned. Details at six o'clock."

At the mention of my mother's name, I whirled to face the television. Mrs. Gummidge made a sound like dishwater going down a drain. Her mouth flapped open. Her eyes grew as round as bubbles, and she peered toward the television as if there might be something more—as if there had been an awful mistake that the announcer would now correct. But the announcer was gone. On the screen, a pair of hands plunged into soapy water and squeaked across clean dishes.

"Oh," said Mrs. Gummidge in a strangled voice. "Dear."

She put her hand over her mouth as if she'd said too much.

"Oh dear," she said again. "And with an election coming up next fall."

I didn't say anything.

"Mr. Sweetwine will be terribly . . . oh dear," she said for the third time. She looked over to see how I was taking it, and I blinked back at her.

"He'll be mad?" I suggested.

"He'll be absolutely . . . I don't suppose he's been informed yet." She stopped and listened. "What was that?"

Far off, in the main part of the house, my mother called.

"She's going to make me dress like them," I reminded Mrs. Gummidge, stepping back until the windowsill pressed into my spine.

"Willa?" My mother came closer. Her heels tapped across the tiles.

Mrs. Gummidge took another long look at my outfit. She was distracted by the incident on the television, but I could see her pulling herself together, forcing herself to concentrate. "I'm thinking," she said. "Could you not dress like the quints just this once? Just to keep things a bit . . . just to make things go a bit smoother . . . for the next little while?"

Something closed up in my throat. I hated her. I made an angry move toward the door, but her voice stopped me.

"Of course, I'd leave those shoes on," she added, "so when we see the photos we'll be sure which girl is *you.*"

I looked down at my bright red high-tops with the sparkly silver laces. The ghost of a grin eased the lump in my throat just as my mother pushed through the heavy door into the staff wing.

"Willa? *There* you are. Goodness, Mrs. Gummidge. I hope she wasn't disturbing you."

Mrs. Gummidge said, "Not at all," and my mother went on, "Willa, we've had *quite* enough of this. You will march yourself upstairs and put on that outfit right now. The photographers have been waiting for twenty minutes already."

As I followed her out, I looked back at Mrs. Gummidge. She was fiddling with her collar, glowering at the television.

"Aren't you going to tell her about the news?" I ventured.

"She's got plenty to worry about," said Mrs. Gummidge. "Don't you go troubling her with this. She'll hear about it soon enough. You hurry along, now."

As for the photos—well, I guess you've seen them. My red high-tops made the front page from coast to coast.

Chapter 4

Mr. Sweetwine exploded. He was in the library, banging things and shouting. Every now and then the door opened and some-one rushed in or out. I caught a glimpse of red Mountie uni-forms and the serious faces of people in dark suits. My mother emerged, hurried across the hallway, and stopped when she saw me peeking over the back of the living room couch.

"What are you doing there?" she asked. Her eyes were red, and she spoke quickly, as though I were keeping her from some-thing.

"Nothing," I said.

"Why don't you go play with the quintuplets?" she said, but I shot her a withering look until she pinched the bridge of her nose.

"The thing is," she said, "we don't know who sent your father's note to the newspaper. It's very upsetting. This kind of thing is very bad for Jordan's image. I don't think you under-stand."

"Yes, I do," I said.

"Then please don't make it harder for me. Not right now. Go on upstairs and find something to do."

I hugged my knees and clenched my teeth.

"I mean it," she said, so I stomped up the stairs.

Eventually, the commotion died down. One by one, the advisers and security guards went away. From the window of my blue room I saw them get into cars and limousines and drive away. By five o'clock, it was deadly quiet at the official residence. Delicious smells of roast chicken and potatoes came from the kitchen, and Mr. Sweetwine and my mother disappeared to have cocktails and dinner with some Very Important People. From behind the door of the quintuplets' room came the sound of muffled laughter. They were in there, playing some dumb game. Not that I cared. I felt ten years older than my new stepsisters, who fluttered and giggled and called their father "Daddy."

I rummaged in the bottom of my suitcase for a couple of bus tickets and five dollars my dad had given me before I left Montreal.

I would have asked Nanny Grayson how to get to the nearest McDonalds, but she had disappeared into the quints' room, and I could hear her through the door. She must be playing their stupid game with them. Anyway, I knew the bus went right down Sussex Drive, and I could ask directions from the bus driver. I didn't think of leaving a note or asking permission or anything.

I just left. The house was terribly quiet. I took the opportunity to slide down the curving bannister of the spiral staircase, which was something I'd been wanting to try ever since I arrived, and it lifted my spirits. But outside the Mounties were gone from the doorstep, and this was a bit of a letdown. A boy from my class at North Centennial Elementary School had once made a Mountie snicker, and I was dying to see if I could do it, too.

It was one of those summer evenings when the traffic sounds distant, the gray clouds press down on the world, and you feel lonely in a sad pleasant way. Everything was damp and solemn. Even the cars on Sussex Drive seemed more dignified than ordinary cars. My feet hardly made a sound on the driveway. When I got to the gate, the Mountie in the security booth jumped up and peered at me through the glass with startled eyes, like a goldfish. He'd been reading a letter. When I knocked on the window, he crushed the pink flowery paper to his chest. Then he poked his head out the door, folding the letter and jamming it clumsily into an envelope. "May I ask where you are going, miss?"

Nobody had ever called me *miss* before. I enjoyed it. I shoved my hands in the back pockets of my jeans.

"McDonalds," I said.

His eyes got rounder than ever. A station wagon slowed suddenly on Sussex Drive, and three or four people goggled at me as they drove by. I scowled at them. They waved.

"You're going to McDonalds?" the Mountie said. "Is that okay with your mother?"

"Yeah," I said, "Of course."

"Nobody advised me," he said in a puzzled voice. "I'll just ring up."

"Why?"

"Just to make sure it's all right."

"I already told you it's all right," I said in my fiercest voice. "I've done it a million times. I'll be back in an hour."

He completely ignored me. He scratched his head and reached for the gatehouse phone. I heard the murmur of his voice behind the glass, and an uncomfortable feeling came over me. Before he'd even hung up, the front door of the official residence flew open and five people dashed out. They peered left and right, spotted us, and charged straight up the driveway. One of them was Nanny Grayson. Two were quintuplets and two were RCMP officers. Their footsteps pounded on the asphalt. I stepped back. The iron railings of the big gate pressed against my back, wet and cold.

"Good heavens," said Nanny Grayson.

"Good heavens," echoed one of the quintuplets.

"Everything under control here, Nick?" asked a big guard with red hair.

The gatehouse Mountie nodded. "Just thought I'd check it out. Sounded a little fishy to me," he said.

"You did the right thing," said the redheaded one. "Good work."

I glared at Nick as hard as I could, and he turned pink. I stood there holding onto the railings, feeling wild and bewildered.

"I'm just going out for a while," I explained. "I'll be back before dinner."

They laughed nervously, and Nanny Grayson said, "You'll do no such thing. Where on earth did you think you were going?"

My heart pounded uncomfortably.

"McDonalds," I said.

The red-haired guard stared for a moment, then let out a guffaw of rude laughter. The others joined in. I heard one of the quintuplets ask the other, "What's McDonalds?"

"Don't tell Mrs. Gummidge," joked Nick, and the others laughed even louder.

This time when I tried to kill him with my piercing gaze, he didn't even notice. Nanny Grayson didn't laugh, but her puzzled tone was even harder to bear than their mocking.

"Are you hungry, Willa? We'll be having dinner soon. If you needed a snack, all you had to do was ask."

"No," I protested. "I'm not hungry. I just wanted to . . ."

Their big grinning faces hung on my words, waiting to laugh again. I closed my fingers so tightly around the gate that my knuckles ached. "Never mind."

"Let's go back to the house," she said. "It's damp out here." The quintuplets trotted like obedient puppies back up the driveway, but Nanny Grayson waited, staring at me until I peeled myself from the fence.

"Thank you, Nick," she said. She looked up at him from under her eyelashes. Her eyes were bright blue, and when she smoothed a strand of hair back from her cheek she went all pink.

Nick just said, "Any time," in a polite way. Then he stood there, looking at her.

"Come on, come on," the quintuplets urged.

By the time we reached the front step, the three officers were hooting again. Their laughter floated across the lawn from the gatehouse. Something terrible twisted inside me. I slammed the front door as hard as I could. The brass knocker clanged alarmingly, and the paintings shivered on the walls of the lower entryway.

"My mother will not be happy about this!" I shouted.

"Probably not," Nanny Grayson agreed with a sigh. "Do you realize you could have caused another scandal? Do you know what the tabloids would do with an incident like that?"

"My mother lets me go where I want," I yelled. "I don't have to ask permission! She trusts me."

"It's not a question of trust," said Nanny Grayson. "In this house, it's a question of security. We can't have you out wandering the streets. It's not safe."

The quintuplets nodded gravely, as if I were too young to understand. This was the worst insult of all. I uttered one of my blackest curses.

"Well," said Nanny Grayson, "That's enough of that. You'd better go to your room, please, until you can control your temper. And your language."

I slammed my door and drifted around and around my cold blue room like a fish in a bowl.

🍁 🍁 🍁

After a while, they called me for dinner.

"I'm not hungry."

Nanny Grayson stood with her hand on my doorknob, sighed, and said, "Well, fine." The door clicked and she went away.

I threw pillows. I kicked the dresser. Everything in that room, from the thick carpet to the heavy drapes, was muffled and polite. I uttered every black curse I could think of. I collected them. I knew one hundred and seventy-three.

Someone tapped on the door.

"I'm not hungry!" I yelled.

The door swung open. Mrs. Gummidge loomed large against the light from the hallway.

"They tell me you will not come down for dinner," she said.

I couldn't think of anything to say. If she had been Nanny Grayson or my mother or even Mr. Sweetwine, I'd have had plenty to say. But there was something about Mrs. Gummidge that made me hold my tongue.

"I have spent the entire afternoon on that chicken," she said. "Your mother told me it was your favorite, and if I do say so, this one will melt in your mouth. I've also made a chocolate mousse for dessert, which you will remember for weeks to come."

I hesitated.

"I have heard about the McDonalds incident," she went on, "which some might call an outrage, considering the effort that was going on in the kitchen just to please you and to make you feel welcome here."

I shifted my attention uncomfortably from her flashing eyes to the crisscross pattern on the bedspread.

"But," she said, "if you'll come down and enjoy this meal,

and thank the kitchen staff nicely afterward, we'll say no more about the whole sordid affair."

The roast chicken smell wafted up the staircase, drifting past Mrs. Gummidge. I swallowed hard.

"Are we having gravy?" I asked.

She sighed deeply and put her hands on her hips. "I'll excuse the question," she said, "because it just shows how much you have to learn about dinners in this house. My chicken gravy has been praised by three heads of state and a senior editor from *Dining Out* magazine. We do not serve roast chicken in this house without the finest of gravy."

She drew a weary breath and swept a strand of hair from her forehead.

"Will you, or will you not, come down to dinner?" she asked.

I did.

🍁 🍁 🍁

After that, things warmed up between Mrs. Gummidge and me. She let me watch *Canada Morning* in her sitting room while she prepared breakfast, and sometimes we stole a few quiet moments for the evening news. One night during the sports segment she explained why the quintuplets had never—except for the half-hour of their father's wedding—been allowed off the grounds of the official residence.

"Let me get this straight," I said. "You mean these kids have never gone past the front gate of this place? Never, ever?"

Mrs. Gummidge gave one of her more expressive sniffs. "You needn't come on like one of those gossip columnists. The little girls are perfectly fine."

"But Gummy, they never went to the beach or on a field trip or to the supermarket or *anything?*"

"You know as well as I do that they can swim right here in their very own pool. Our schoolroom—*your* schoolroom, I might point out—is the best in the whole country. And has it slipped your mind, miss, that in this house *some* people make their living choosing the food you eat? What would those children do in a supermarket?"

A long list of hockey scores scrolled up the television screen. Some of the kitchen staff laughed and teased each other in the pantry.

"And I'll thank you to call me by my proper name, if it wouldn't be too much trouble," she added tartly.

"I heard the others. . . ."

"I am *quite* aware of the family nickname."

A weather map appeared on the screen. A smiling woman passed her hand over the whole country.

"I still don't understand *why,*" I said.

"For pity's sake, it's just a short form of Mrs. Gummidge!" she snapped. "They called me Gummy when they were babies and the name stuck, that's all!"

"I meant I don't understand about *the quints,*" I said. "And why their father never lets them out."

Mrs. Gummidge snorted and settled deeper into her chair and said, "Oh, for pity's sake."

"Could the quints go out if they *wanted* to?" I persisted.

"They *don't* want to. And don't you go putting crazy ideas in their heads, do you hear me?"

"But if they *wanted* to . . ."

She sat straight up, put her feet on the floor, and leaned toward me. The weather woman's map cast a strange blue glow on the side of Mrs. Gummidge's face.

"They're *safe* here," she said. "We had that little trouble when they were small, but they've been *safe* here for years. Do you understand?"

I gulped. "What trouble?"

She glanced away as if she'd already said too much. "Intruders. When they were two," she confessed. "It was terrible." She closed her eyes. Then she opened them and said, "Some candid photos got into the *National Tattletale*. Someone managed to hide a camera inside a teddy bear and snap a whole roll of pictures of the children."

She swallowed and went on. "We never knew who did it. Mr. Sweetwine kept saying that anyone who could get a camera onto the grounds could also smuggle in a gun. The children are just too famous—we began to worry about them day and night. Mr. Sweetwine improved our security systems, but we've been afraid of kidnappers ever since. We've never forgotten that incident. You have no idea."

"Kidnappers," I said.

She sat back in the chair and pulled the sweater more

warmly around her shoulders. "There. I've gone and said too much."

The weather woman let out another jolly laugh. Mrs. Gummidge turned her face away from me.

"You've nothing to fear," she said. "You're perfectly safe as long as you're here inside the fence."

That's how I came to understand about scandals and kidnappers. They haunted the people in that house the way fire haunts people who work in a dynamite factory, the way icebergs terrify people who work on cruise ships, the way tornadoes make it hard for people in trailer parks to go to sleep.

"Well, never mind. I'm not worried about it," I promised. And I wasn't. Actually, I was worried about something else entirely.

Chapter 5

If you can picture a wild sunflower bursting into an English rose garden, you'll have some inkling of what it felt like for me to arrive in that household.

Of course, my mother had always been a rose. Everybody could see that right away. She leaned toward the quintuplets, and they lifted their perfect faces toward her. I kept coming across little clusters of identical sisters engaged in *tête-à-têtes* with my mother while silver light and delicate laughter seemed to fall over everything.

In that house I would catch my mother looking at me with a puzzled expression, like a swan who has hatched out a woodpecker. It was hard to understand why the quintuplets had more of her swanlike gracefulness than I did.

"I wish somebody *would* kidnap them," I muttered darkly to Mrs. Gummidge, who was so shocked that she wouldn't speak to me for the rest of the day.

I missed my father. The expensive hush of the official residence, with its family asleep in their tidy rooms, closed around me, and I was so lonely. Sometimes it got so bad I would sit straight up in bed. When you're the only one awake in a house full of sleeping celebrities, the loneliness grabs you around the middle and squeezes you hard.

One night it got so bad I felt as if there were eyes and ghosts and enemy soldiers in my room.

I scurried out into the hallway. When I got to the shiny bathroom at the end of the hall I stopped and stared at myself in the mirror. Against the elegant gray tiles and big fluffy towels, with everything gleaming so hard it hurt my eyes, I felt like a dandelion, white and puffy with seeds, waiting for a sudden breeze to scatter me. I studied myself until my face in the mirror seemed to grow huge. Then it swooped dizzily away again.

That's when I heard a door open and close. That was all—just the slip of a door latch, a pause, and then a click as it shut tight again.

When I peeked into the hallway, everything was silent and still. I should have gone back to bed. But I didn't. I snapped off the lights and lingered in the bathroom with the door ajar.

The sound of squeaking hinges was like the moan of a werewolf in the deep night. The swish of someone crossing the hall was like the sighing of a ghost.

A couple of meters to my right, a heavy door—the one which leads up to the staff quarters—was swinging shut. All I saw before it closed was the flash of someone's heel as the person melted up the shadowy stairs.

I shoved my face hard against the towel rack until I was absolutely sure the mysterious intruder was gone. Then I scurried back to my room, shut the door, dragged the night table in front of it, and threw myself into bed. I have a lot of respect for those girl sleuths you sometimes read about. Until you've actually encountered a sinister figure in the dead of night, you can't really appreciate how safe and comfortable you are in your own bed.

I pulled the covers tight around me, clutched my pillow, and lay straining my ears against the terrible silence until a dizzy sleep dipped down and enveloped me.

Chapter 6

On the telephone, my father sounded cheerful. He didn't sound like the same dad who had taken to phoning the prime minister's official residence every couple of hours just to ask how things were going.

I knew about the phone calls because my mother had finally ordered the staff to screen them out, and Mr. Sweetwine kept making jokes about how we would need a full-time receptionist just to handle the Howard Problem.

This created in my mind the idea that my father must be wallowing and stumbling in a black pit of despair.

So I phoned him. When he answered I thought for a moment that I had dialed a wrong number.

"Willie!" he trumpeted. "Hello!"

I wondered if any customers happened to be in the flower shop. I pictured them lingering over the jonquils, wasting time so they could eavesdrop on my father's conversation.

"I'm *so* glad you called!" he bellowed.

When my father answered the phone, everyone within earshot received the benefit of his surprise and enthusiasm. You could practically see the happy sound waves spreading out from his cubbyhole near the cash register, spilling through the back garden and out over the train tracks and booming out the front door in a blast of good will.

"How's your mother? How are you? How are things *going* there?"

"Everything's fine, Dad. I just . . . well, I just . . . wanted to call."

"Good for you, Willie. That's *good!* How's your mother?"

"She's fine."

"She got the bouquet?"

"Yes."

"And the card? She got the card?"

"Yes."

"Don't have to tell me, eh, Willie?" he demanded with a hearty guffaw. "I've had reporters here—did you see me on the news? Did you read about me in the paper? I'm getting to be quite the celebrity, wouldn't you say?"

I badly wanted to change the subject.

"What are you inventing these days, Dad?"

"Knot-resistant shoelaces," he recited as if they did not interest him. "Self-trimming cedar hedges. Modelling dough that changes colors when you squish it."

"I'd like to see that."

"What a terrific idea! Come as soon as you can! Come today!"

"I can't." My voice came out flat. "They won't let me."

"What do you mean? Of course they'll let you! Let me speak to your mother!"

"No, Dad."

"What do you mean, no?"

"She says it's too soon. She says I have to try and get used to living here first."

"Ridiculous." In one way his shouting and sputtering made me feel better, but in another way it made me as restless and uncomfortable as a wet cat. "Let me speak to her!" he yelled. "Put her on the line!"

"I can't, Dad. She's not even here. She's gone next door to some reception at the French embassy."

He grunted. He sounded like a jealous lion grumbling over its dinner. He muttered and cleared his throat. I could picture him straightening the worn collar of his tweedy old sweater.

"You'll come soon," he promised. "I'll talk it over with her."

"Dad, I don't think she really wants to . . ."

"Wants to *what?*"

"Well, talk anything over with you." I wrapped the phone cord so tightly around my fingers they turned purple. "I think she likes it here."

"Oh, Willie," he said in a more subdued voice. "Don't worry. She's just dazzled by all that money and fame. It won't be long before she realizes she was happier here with me. He might be rich and powerful, but he can't offer her what she *really* wants."

"What do you mean?"

"Romance!" hollered my father. "Genuine, extravagant, from-the-heart romance! I'll win her over. You can count on that!"

"Dad?"

I tried to interrupt, but he was in full voice. He didn't even hear me.

"Imagination!" he crowed. "That's what she needs! And I've got it in buckets. In barrels, Willie. Imagination and a loving heart. He doesn't stand a chance against that. Not a *chance!*"

"Dad?"

"Yes?"

"I was just wondering why . . . I mean, how come . . . well, Mom and I moved to Ottawa three years ago and in all that time you never tried to get her back."

"Simple!" he yelped. "I was waiting for her to realize her mistake!"

"What?"

"She didn't really want to be independent, Willie. She only thought she did. I was waiting for her to realize that. I knew she would realize her mistake and come back to me."

"But—"

"And she *would* have. She was right on the brink of it when *he* got in the way. It confused her."

"Oh," I said.

"Willie, you're so young. You don't understand these things."

"Dad . . ."

"I've already planned some really beautiful romantic gestures. Really irresistible. And if you promise not to tell anyone . . ."

"What?"

"I'm working on a very special project that she will absolutely not be able to resist. I can guarantee that."

"What is it?"

"Top secret, Willie. But I promise you, it's grand. It's whimsical. It's gorgeous."

"Oh."

"Don't worry, my little sidekick. We'll soon have our family back together again."

I didn't say anything.

"You'll come for a visit. Real soon," he promised. "I'll talk to her."

"Thanks," I said and changed the subject. I told him all about my room, Mrs. Gummidge, and the quintuplets.

But after I hung up, all I could think about was my crazy lonely dad and his big romantic gestures. It made me more restless than ever.

Chapter 7

The next morning, before lessons, I asked one of the quintuplets, "Wouldn't you like to wear this green scarf?"

"Thank you," said the quintuplet in that super-polite way of theirs, "but I really don't think it would match my navy jumper."

"As if *that* matters." I flung the scarf around my throat and gathered handfuls of it to my face. "It feels just like water—cool and smooth. And it's green as . . . green as *algae.*"

"Well, thank you anyway," replied the quint, buttoning her crisp white collar.

"You always dress like your sisters, don't you?" I had been through this before, with a couple of the other quints (or maybe I was having this conversation for the third time with the *same* quint—it was hard to tell). I tumbled backward onto the bed and stretched luxuriously, drawing deep breaths through the scarf.

"We almost always dress alike," the quint admitted patiently.

"Why?"

"Well, because we've always done it. And because the photographers like it when we all look the same. It makes us, I don't know, special."

"Special as a *group,*" I said. "Special as *quintuplets,* eh?"

She eyed me strangely. "What do you mean?"

"I mean," I went on, sitting up, "what makes *you* special? As a person, I mean. You, yourself." I leaned forward. "For example, I'm sitting here talking to you, and *I don't even know which one you are.* Do you see what I mean?"

She gazed at me for a long moment.

"I'm Suzanne," she said at last.

"Aughhh!" I threw myself back on the bed and drew mournful breaths of scarf. "My mother wore this to that cocktail party last night. I can smell her perfume in it."

Suzanne stared.

"We have to go to the schoolroom now," she said. "They'll be expecting us."

I lay still with the scarf over my face. "I'm a corpse," I said, "and this is my shroud."

She pondered this. "By any chance, did you ask your mother's permission to take that scarf?"

When I didn't answer, she said, "Oh well. It's none of my business." There was a long, long pause. Finally, as she turned to leave, I let my breath explode out, puffing the scarf from my face.

"I wasn't ignoring you," I panted. "I thought if I held my breath long enough I might have an out-of-body experience, but all I saw were a bunch of sparkly lights. Okay. Time for school."

🍁 🍁 🍁

The schoolroom was in the basement. We learned the significant dates in the life of Matisse, the principles and practices of the Geneva Convention, and the formula for calculating *pi*. It was not my idea of a superior education, and I said so. At North Centennial Elementary School, this would have been allowed.

"I don't understand," I said, "how you can lock five kids in a house for eleven years and give them this stuff and expect them to know how to *live.*"

They were all baffled, even Nanny Grayson. But the mood in the official residence has a way of pulling people into its spell, and they all looked at me as if I'd proposed to burn the place down.

I knew the freckles were standing out in my face, and I became uncomfortably aware that the green of the scarf at my throat was not my best color. (You may remember that seafoam-green was the color chosen for the bridesmaids' dresses at my mother's wedding because it suited the quints to perfection. On me, it created an unfortunate rumpled effect, which you may have noticed.)

I faced those blank expressions.

"Girls," said Nanny Grayson. "Ladies."

For once, maybe for the first time ever, the obedient faces of the quintuplets didn't swivel automatically toward her voice. Five pairs of startled brown eyes continued to drill into me.

I turned to the nearest quintuplet and asked, "I mean, what do you want to *be?*"

She didn't understand the question.

"What will you do when you grow up? How will you live? Who will you be?"

"Well," she said in a sprightly voice. "We're going to be ambassadors of good will."

This answer silenced even me for a long moment.

"What *is* that?" I asked.

The quintuplet looked vaguely puzzled, like someone working out a math problem. Then she shrugged. "I don't know, exactly."

"Then how do you know you want to be one?" I yelled, but the quintuplet was ready with the best answer of all.

"Oh, because Daddy said so."

🍁 🍁 🍁

"I wish someone *would* kidnap them," I growled again that night, and Mrs. Gummidge humphed and hunched her shoulders and glowered at me.

"I'll thank you to stop saying such dreadful things. You ought to count your lucky stars. That's all I'm going to say. You don't even know what you're talking about."

Then she told me how the quintuplets had worn homing devices under their bridesmaid dresses during our brisk trot down the aisle and how security was so tight at the official residence that guards walked around inside the house all night and how she would harm her own *self* before she'd let anyone touch a hair on the heads of the Sweetwine children—and that included me. She said we were the light of her life, the wind in her sails, the blossoms on her African violets.

She got quite worked up during this speech. When she finally stopped, her cheeks were pink and she was out of breath.

She turned her attention back to the letter she was writing.

"That's all I have to say," she said. "You just count your blessings. You're safe here. There'll be no more talk of kidnappers in this house."

And, of course, there wasn't. At least, not *that* night.

Chapter 8

I found my mother in the sunroom, which overlooks the wide green lawn of the official residence and the river beyond. She was curled up in a wicker chair with her feet under her, like a girl, writing busily on a clipboard. When I came in, she gave me a weary smile and chewed the end of her pen.

"I'm planning out the flower beds for the fall planting," she said. "I want the gardener to order the bulbs next week."

The thought of being around for the fall planting did not lift my spirits. I perched on a footstool beside her and cleared my throat.

"It's about Dad," I said.

"Oh dear." She crossed out the kidney-shaped bed of daffodils she had sketched, and I felt as if I had just killed off two hundred innocent little flowers.

"I see," she said at last. She put on her psychologist-mother mask. "What about him?"

"I want to go see him," I said. A bubble of worry inflated in my chest as she pretended my words hadn't hurt her. She frowned over the clipboard, doodled a couple of tulips, and set her lips tightly together.

"I see," she said again. "Is there any chance I can convince you to wait a few weeks?"

The bubble grew and grew inside me, pressing so hard that my throat tightened and my breath seemed to ache.

"Why?" I asked.

"Well," she said, "you haven't been here very long. If you go to your dad's place now, it might look as if you don't like

41

your new family. It could create a wrong impression."

I gave her a look implying that the impression created would not be as wrong as she thought. But she was being so reasonable, so calm and professional, that a black curse began to hammer inside me.

"You haven't even given it a chance," she went on. "Why don't you get to know your new sisters a bit first? Settle into your room. Things like that."

"I want to go stay with Dad."

Her face twisted. The curses banged like stones inside me, hammering to come out.

"I'm just asking," I said in a wobbly voice. "It doesn't mean I . . . It doesn't mean anything. . . ."

She rubbed the back of her neck.

"I'll speak to Jordan," she said. "You're not making this easy for me. You know that."

The way she bent her head over the clipboard and pursed her lips, I knew I'd been dismissed.

🍁 🍁 🍁

As soon as my mother emerged from the prime minister's office, I could tell that things hadn't gone well. Her eyes were hard, almost sarcastic, and she plunged her hands deep into the pockets of her linen jacket.

I reached under the cuff of my jeans and scratched the side of my ankle, where I'd drawn a fake tattoo with a ballpoint pen—it was very beautiful, a moon and stars of my own design. My mother hadn't noticed it yet.

"He wants to see you," she said.

I blinked. "What for?"

"I don't know. You'll have to ask him."

I wasn't worried. I am a good arguer, as my mother knows, and I thought I could handle any reasons the prime minister might have for keeping me away from my father. The only thing I wasn't prepared for was the one thing he said.

"Absolutely not."

I stared at him for such a long time that he sighed and rubbed his hair.

"I won't even consider it," he said, obviously irritated.

"Why?"

"I'm not prepared to discuss it with you."

"Is it because you want to keep your kids locked up?"

"I *beg* your pardon?"

I stared again. He stood up and began to prowl around his office, sighing and rumpling his hair.

"Nobody in this house is 'locked up.' Let's get that straight," he said. "You're just a child. You don't know the first thing about it."

"Maybe you think the quintuplets don't care," I said, ignoring the insult, "because they've never been out before."

He drilled me with a sharp glance.

"But I *do* care," I went on. "I'm not going to be locked up in this place. I want to see my father. I should be allowed to see him."

"Nobody said you would not be allowed," he said uneasily.

"You said 'absolutely not.' You and my mother are afraid it would be bad for your image. You think it might make more trouble in the newspapers."

He was furious. A crimson flush rushed into his face. He swallowed hard and controlled his voice.

He said softly, "It's just not a good time right now."

"Well, when *will* it be a good time?"

"I don't know!" he exploded. Immediately he looked sorry.

He came around the desk and leaned against a chair with his hands dangling helplessly in his lap.

"Look," he said. "We're not getting off to a very good start. I didn't mean to yell at you."

"Well, I know you're not used to kids like me."

He grinned feebly and went on. "I love your mother very much, and I want us all to be happy together. I don't feel you've given us much of a chance. It sounds as if you've already made up your mind to go live with your father."

"I just want to go there for one week," I said. "There isn't room for *all* the quints at my dad's place, but if a *couple* of them come with me, it won't look like I'm running away or anything. It will look like we're getting along really well."

He didn't say anything.

"You're afraid they're going to get kidnapped," I said.

"Willa!"

"But it would be a big secret—this visit," I promised. "We wouldn't tell anybody except my father."

He thought hard.

"The quints would love it. It would be good for them," I pressed on. "And the public would love to hear about it, too."

He was looking at me. Reading me as if I were a newspaper.

"I'm sure it would make you look really good in the opinion polls," I went on. "On the other hand, if people thought you were keeping me away from my father it might look . . . well, bad."

He fixed me with a hard look. I'd seen him on the news, a few times, yelling at members of the opposition party. For a moment I thought I was going to get a real-life demonstration of his temper.

Then he got himself under control. "Let me think about it. I won't say yes right away. And you're not to say anything to anyone in the meantime."

"Okay," I promised. "You can count on me."

This time he grinned as if he couldn't help himself. I grinned back. For a moment there was a kind of camaraderie between us. Then the phone rang, and he grew businesslike again, humphing into the receiver and scribbling notes with his gold pen.

I let myself quietly out of the office.

🍁 🍁 🍁

The next afternoon we were summoned into his presence again—Anne, Diane and me. My mother had chosen them. She had actually fretted over them, studying each quintuplet to see which ones would benefit most from this little field trip—which ones would get along well together and with me and with my dad.

"What difference does it make?" I demanded, as she considered one after the other. "They're all the *same.*"

"Maybe if you spent some time with them," she said, "you'd discover how wrong you are."

But I had no idea what she was talking about.

So Anne and Diane and I waited at the top of the spiral staircase outside the prime minister's office for fifteen minutes while my mother was in there, discussing things with him. Now and then I could hear the murmur of voices.

Anne grilled me for more information. "Did you say you

used to go on the bus by yourself? Do you think we could go on a bus?"

"Yes, do you?" Diane echoed. "I don't know. I might be a bit scared."

"*She* could come with us." Anne gestured at me, and I scowled.

"I'm not your servant, you know. Everybody in the world is not your servant."

My mother opened the door just in time to prevent a real fight.

"You three may come in," she said.

"Thank you." That was Anne, as if it were nothing at all, being ushered into her father's presence.

"What's this I hear?" asked Mr. Sweetwine in his most fatherly manner.

"Daddy, can we go? Please?" Anne leaned across the enormous desk and gazed adoringly into her father's face. She stroked his expensive sleeve. Diane sat on the edge of a desk chair and added the voltage of her pleading eyes to Anne's. The total effect was extremely powerful and seemed to have a mesmerizing effect on Mr. Sweetwine. I could just imagine what would happen if five of them decided to do it at the same time.

"Ho-ho . . . well, now," he said.

I hitched myself up on the edge of a low bookcase and sat swinging my feet.

"Young Willa has already spoken to me about this," he said in a jovial voice. "Isn't that right?"

"Yes." I swung my left foot sideways so he would have a better view of my tattoo. He did not seem to notice it. "I'd love it if they could come with me," I said. "Sir."

My mother stared as if I were a new species of weed.

"And, my own good girls, would you like to go?" Mr. Sweetwine went on, enjoying his fatherly role.

"Yes, Daddy," Diane said. "Please."

"Well." Mr. Sweetwine was at the height of his joviality. He practically swelled. "If only it were this easy to run the country, eh? Everybody gets what they want."

"I don't." That was my mother.

The stab of guilt was like a knife twisting inside me. I stopped swinging my foot. My hands shook.

"And what do you want, Louise?" Mr. Sweetwine's gaze always softened when he looked at my mother.

"I would rather see you try to get along here," said my mother to me. "But I won't stand in your way. I just want you to know how I feel about it."

"Hooray," said Anne in a soft thrilled voice. It was the kind of thing that melts adults. I, myself, had never mastered it, although I could see how powerful it was when used at the right moment. Mr. Sweetwine melted, and even my mother showered doting glances on the pair of quintuplets.

"All right, then," said Mr. Sweetwine. "I'll approve the security measures myself. This is to be absolutely, totally secret, do you understand? Not a soul is to know about this visit. I won't sleep a wink until you're home again."

"We promise, Daddy," said Anne.

"Yes, we promise," said Diane, and I knew he could count on them. After all, they didn't know a soul outside the official residence. Who did he think they were going to tell?

Chapter 9

A few days later, I spoke to my father, who was complaining bitterly that a team of security agents had combed through his flower shop, his apartment, and his garden, leaving a complicated list of procedures for him to follow before our arrival. There were locks and alarms to be installed. Special bars had to be put on the windows and buzzers on the doors.

"Just so my own daughter can visit me," he fumed. "I'm outraged."

"Me, too. I'm outraged," I agreed. "But really, it's nothing to do with me. It's to protect the quints."

"The what?"

"The quints. The quintuplets."

"For heaven's sake. You make them sound like jam. Quince. What's all this hullabaloo? Is this how they run your life, now?"

"I guess so. They're afraid the quints will be kidnapped."

"For heaven's sake," he said again.

"I know."

"You're only bringing *two* of them."

"I know."

"Well, what would be the point of kidnapping *two?* If I were a kidnapper, I'd want the whole set, wouldn't you?"

"Dad!"

"What?"

"Don't even joke about that. They're really sensitive about that kind of stuff."

"Well, think about it," he persisted. "It would be like stealing two volumes of an encyclopedia. What would be the point?" I laughed in spite of myself. On the other end of the line, my father sighed and said, "I miss you, Willie."

"I miss you too, Dad."

I lowered my voice as I said it, to make sure my mother wouldn't hear. The familiar old mixture of happiness, sadness, and guilt washed over me.

I looked around the clean empty hallway with the expensive paintings hanging against the creamy wallpaper and tried to picture my father. He would be perched on the old stool in his cluttered shop, leaning his elbows on the counter.

"I'll see you soon, Dad."

"Sure, Willie. We'll have a good time."

🍁 🍁 🍁

It was after midnight when I awoke to the loneliness of my blue room. The big famous house was silent. I had been dreaming about Lucinda Dooley, who went to Hollywood to become a movie star and took her whole family with her. I started toward the bathroom to get a drink of water.

I always enjoyed the way you could creep up and down the hallways of the official residence without making a sound. The carpet was so thick my bare feet seemed to disappear into it. I could have used the quints' bathroom, but I preferred the bathroom at the other end of the hall.

That's when I saw her. I know you'll think I'm making this up—hindsight and all that—but I swear a chill ran right down my spine, the way it does in mystery novels when the girl detective first spots the culprit.

She was creeping from the big playroom toward the stairs that lead up to the rooms where the live-in staff sleep. She really was creeping—not just enjoying the deep carpet the way I was, but trying hard not to be seen. She was trying to make herself as invisible as a shadow against the darker shadows of the hallway.

I stopped. Took two steps back toward my room. Stopped again and held perfectly still.

She didn't see me. She was so intent on creeping, holding the heavy door as she slid through and easing it shut behind her, that she never saw me.

But I tell you, right at that very moment, I knew there was something spooky going on.

It was Nanny Grayson, and she was up to no good.

🍁 🍁 🍁

About an hour before we got to Montreal, I began to worry. Anne, Diane, and I were wedged in the back seat of the limousine between Nick—the gatehouse guard who had laughed at me—and another bodyguard. I was wondering what this visit would really be like. I realized I had never pictured Anne and Diane in the shop, the apartment, or the garden. It's not as if I thought they would mysteriously disappear. I just never thought of them at all. As for the bodyguards, I had no idea where they were going to stay. Until we were actually in the car, clamped between them like books between bookends, I never even thought of them as real people.

I don't know what I was expecting. Maybe I thought my father would come down the steps from the shop, giving us a welcoming smile and saying, "I was going to put the kettle on for tea, but I forgot to buy tea. Come in and have some ginger ale."

By the time we left the autoroute, Anne and Diane were looking white and scared, and I was beginning to feel the same way. When we turned onto Sherbrooke Street, Anne began to pester me with questions: "Is this where you used to live? . . . Do you know any of these people? . . . Is that where you used to buy your food? . . . Do you think anybody is recognizing us?"

"Nobody recognizes you," I snapped, as the driver waited for a red light to change. "Nobody is even looking at you. Nobody even *cares* about you."

"That's good," she said in a doubting voice.

On my father's street, there was a commotion. Nick and the other bodyguard sat up straight and shot meaningful looks at each other.

"Trouble," said Nick.

"Yeah," said the other guard.

The street was jammed with cars. People milled about on the sidewalk. The flashing lights of police cars reflected off every storefront.

"What's happening?" asked Diane nervously.

"Probably a sidewalk sale," I said. "Or a fender bender."

"A what?"

"She means a car accident," said Anne.

"Gosh."

I just smirked. To tell you the truth, I was nervous.

It was impossible to manoeuvre the sleek black car through the uproar on the street, and the bodyguards had no intention of letting us get out and walk. They talked together busily, importantly. They listened to radio transmissions on the special, hardly noticeable hearing devices that fitted right into their ears. Now and then, one or the other would suddenly stop talking, clap one hand to the side of his head, and get a fiercely intent look on his face.

"Looks like a deerfly just crawled in his ear," I observed. The hysterically funny nature of this comment was lost on Anne and Diane.

"What's wrong?" Anne demanded.

"Yeah," echoed Diane. "What's going on?"

"Official business or something," I said. "I don't know. Anyway, what are you so worried about? We're sitting here in a bulletproof car with tinted glass windows, wearing homing devices, between two bodyguards with radios and, for all we know, guns. I mean, what do you think is going to happen to us?"

What *did* happen was that my father suddenly appeared out of the crowd with his anxious hair blowing around. He wrung his hands, shouldered his way to our car, and peered in. He squinted at the reflection of his own worried face in the tinted glass.

There was a moment of silence. My father was making wild gestures with one arm, which caused the guards to exchange grim looks.

"Who is this crackpot?" asked Nick.

"That's my dad," I said. "He's asking you to roll down the window."

But my father had given up the charade. He began tapping on the glass.

"Oh dear," said Anne. "A lot of people are coming over here. Oh dear. Oh dear."

It was impressive. One minute my father was rapping on the window in relative peace. A moment later he disappeared into a tidal wave of excited smiles. Suddenly, everybody was knocking on the car. We were surrounded by peering eyes and flashing knuckles.

"Cool," I said.

"Make them stop. Make them stop!" Diane sobbed. "I don't like it."

I actually felt sorry for her. Until that moment, I hadn't realized how frightened those kids were.

"They won't hurt us!" I said. "Most of them are my dad's neighbors. That's Madame Tremblay. That kid with the hat is Nigel Labelle—he was in my kindergarten class. The redhead is Gretchen Williamson."

My father forced his way back to our window. The agent lowered it a crack.

"Oooh!" the crowd roared. "Hello! Bonjour!"

Everyone surged forward again. My father said "oof" in a good-natured way and flattened his hands against the car to keep from being crushed.

"Dad, hi! What's going on?"

". . . invited a few friends . . ." He oofed again and let out a grunt. "Told them to keep it quiet. I had no idea."

"Mr. Whimsey," said Nick. "I thought we had a clear agreement about the secrecy of this mission."

My father stared blankly. Someone shoved him from behind, and his shirt bumped the window. His buttons clicked against the glass. "This is not a mission," he said. "It's a father–daughter visit."

"Whatever you call it," Nick said, "it was supposed to be kept completely secret."

". . . a few close friends," my father gasped. "Monsieur Boudreau, you're on my foot."

"Ooh! *Cherie!*" A set of fingertips waggled at me through the crack. *"Ça va?"*

"Hi, Madame Tremblay." There was no time to say anything else.

"Get us out of here," said Nick to the driver.

"Wait a minute!" I cried. "At least drop me off! Where are you taking me? What about my dad?"

"He knew the rules," said Nick. "He couldn't be trusted."

"I'm supposed to stay here for a week!" I yelled. "Mr. Sweetwine will kill you if you take me back to Ottawa."

He merely raised an eyebrow.

"I *mean* it!" I raged. "You'd better let me stay with my dad or I'll . . . I'll . . ."

He raised the other eyebrow.

"You'll be sorry!" I hollered.

"Okay," he said pleasantly, and there was nothing to do but sob horribly all the way home, swiping at the hot tears with the back of my hand.

* * *

My mother reacted as if someone had really tried to hurt us. This surprised me. Not long ago, I used to ride the bus home from school, leave a note, hang out in the computer store at the mall, grab some dinner with Mrs. Vereen at the travel agency (while looking at travel brochures and planning pretend holidays), and get home at nine-thirty. My mother did not worry about me. We used to gossip over tea at bedtime, and the only kidnappers we ever thought about were the bad guys in the Monday mystery movie.

So it surprised me to be enveloped in parental hugs of a frantic nature.

"Are you all right? You're sure you're all right? It's all my fault. I should never have allowed it. I'm so sorry." My mother was so angry she was shaking. Her voice had an edge of tears in it. "I could just *kill* Howard for this. Of all the stupid, childish, pathetic schemes . . ."

"Don't!" I pleaded.

Her words were poisoning the warm fuzziness of the moment, which I'll admit I was enjoying, even though her necklace was making a dent the shape of a cameo in my face.

"It was only Madame Tremblay and Gretchen and Nigel." I protested.

"And about seventy others, according to reports," she said. "Do you realize how frightened Anne and Diane must have been?"

I did. They hadn't actually cried, but their dark eyes grew huge. Anne stroked her father's sleeve as if to reassure him. Diane's lip trembled and Nanny Grayson hugged her.

"Lord knows what the press will make of this," my mother went on in a worried voice. Nanny gave her a look of sympathy and patted Diane's back.

At the same time, my heart was wrenching with a terrible grief. If only they'd let me out of the car. It would have been a wonderful rowdy party, full of familiar faces. Even now, people were probably arguing in my father's garden, crowding into the flower shop and laughing and drinking in his kitchen. And it was all happening without me.

"I'm going upstairs," I said.

Mr. Sweetwine squeezed my shoulder roughly as I pushed past him. I couldn't keep the anger from spilling over.

"You could have let me stay there," I said bitterly.

"It's better this way," he answered.

I tore myself out of his grasp and ran up the stairs two at a time. Behind me, his voice sounded like a feeble afterthought: "I'm sorry it didn't work out."

I slammed my door so hard the wall shuddered. Then the silence settled around me, and I was free to rage and grieve about everything I'd missed.

Chapter 10

I was in the sunroom with the quints. We were halfway through a nice, well-behaved, quintuplet-ish game of Monopoly. My mother had peeked in at us, smiled a benevolent smile, and gone away to do a bit of gardening. Everything was soft and golden. Earlier, a photographer had scurried around, taking pictures as we played the game, and I felt as flat and unreal as an insect squeezed between the shiny pages of a coffee-table book.

"Daddy says the visit to your father was an unmitigated disaster," said Anne.

I didn't say anything.

"That means there was not one good thing about it," she went on. She had received so much attention over the whole thing and was making herself out to be so much more worldly than her sisters that I don't think the disaster could have been nearly as unmitigated as she was letting on.

"Unmitigated disaster," I repeated to no one in particular. "Inexcusable breach of security. Unconscionable." Mr. Sweetwine's vocabulary was full of these gems. I loved the words themselves, but I hated the way he used them to refer to my father.

The quintuplets exchanged sly glances with one another. They thought I was showing off again. Not that I cared. Not that I wasted my time thinking about *them*.

Except that later I lay in bed trying to ignore the uncomfortable feeling that the quints didn't like me. If you'd asked, I would have said I didn't care what happened to the quints. I didn't even like them very much, but I lay between the crisp sheets in my cool bed and wondered whether they were saying bad things about me. I imagined what it would be like in their room, where the five of them would be giggling under their breaths, saying things like, "And did you *see* how she buttoned her shirt wrong this morning? Isn't she the worst *slob* you ever saw?"

I worried that my mother might hear them and go in to hush them and sit on the edge of a bed talking quietly and sharing a joke. For a moment I imagined I could hear their stifled laughter, and I felt lonelier than ever.

I guess that's how I came up with the idea of Games. Every time I closed my eyes, I felt myself swimming around and around inside my room, bumping against the walls like a clumsy catfish.

I twisted restlessly under the covers. If only we could get out. If only our days weren't made up of blackboards and textbooks and polite board games. I wondered what Anne would have been like if she had been just another kid at North Centennial Elementary School.

I lay awake for a long time thinking about it.

The click of the closing door was not a sound that would normally strike terror into the heart of a kid like me. It was distant and discreet, like everything else in that house. But it brought back the memory of Nanny Grayson, sliding along the corridor wall like a shadow while I crouched silently and peered into the darkness.

The sound of the closing door chilled me.

I hadn't said a word to anyone about the way Nanny Grayson had been sneaking around the halls after midnight. To tell you the truth, I'd forgotten all about it. But now, as I slipped out of bed and opened the door just enough to see into the corridor, I wished I hadn't been quite so casual about it.

She stood in the hall with her back to me, deep in whispered conversation with someone half-hidden behind the playroom door. The rest of the house was quiet—the kind of deadly quiet that meant the family were all asleep.

With my fingers cramping tight around the doorknob and the breath aching in the back of my throat, I yearned for my mother or even a sleepy quintuplet to wander into the dark hallway. I strained my ears to hear what Nanny Grayson was saying.

I strained so hard that little lights seemed to dance in front of my eyes. And even as I was listening, I wondered if I might be dreaming.

I thought I heard Nanny Grayson say, "I'm sure they don't suspect a thing."

And a man answered in a deep thrumming voice, "Yeah." It was Nick. Although I couldn't see his face, his voice was familiar, and I caught a glimpse of his hand as he reached up to rub the back of his neck. "But maybe not for long. Look, Pauline. These blackmail threats might be coming from the new kid."

"I thought of that, too. She's unhappy. She might be trying to get attention. If she is the one threatening us, we'll be all right. She'd never follow through."

"If it was just the threat, and the idea that she knows what we're up to, I wouldn't care," he said. "I'd think she was trying to get revenge for that fiasco in Montreal. . . . Shh. . . . Did you hear something?"

They were silent, turning their heads, listening. I stopped breathing. After a moment, Nanny laughed in a low voice and said, "Don't be so nervous. Stop worrying. I can handle Willa."

"You don't think I should quit my job, then?"

Nanny laughed again. "That would be overreacting."

"She seems to know enough to incriminate us."

"Don't worry, Nick. It will be all right."

The rest of the conversation, in whispers, was no louder than the wings of a mosquito against a window screen.

I should have alerted the household. I should have edged up to the culprits, making them jump in fear, and asked fake-innocent questions like, "Why, Nanny Grayson, what are you doing up here this time of night?" until they realized their evil plot had been uncovered.

But I didn't.

I was too scared.

I clung to the doorknob so hard that my fingers ached all the next day. I held my breath so long I thought I might pass out. And when Nanny Grayson slipped back down the corridor, so close I could feel the swish of air from her skirt and catch a trace of the end-of-the-day scent of her perfume, I was overcome by a sudden terror that she would look into my room and find me crouching there, spying.

She'd been gone for several minutes before I heard the click of the door to the servants' wing. Nick disappeared up the stairs.

When I crawled back into bed, I was actually shivering. I pulled the covers right up and listened to my teeth chattering in the dark. I lay awake trying to think of a way to tell my mother what I had overheard without bringing on the weary tone of voice that turned everything I said into some kind of problem.

In the end I decided to say nothing. And by morning, when the sun streamed so cheerfully through the expensive curtains, I was busy with more important things. I was ready to introduce the Sweetwine quintuplets to the real world.

🍁 🍁 🍁

I requested a meeting with the prime minister. I did it in writing, and after he received the memo Mr. Sweetwine told Nanny Grayson that I was going to fit very nicely into this household.

The meeting was set for 6:30 P.M. As soon as the staff had cleared the dinner dishes, I went into the library with Mr. Sweetwine. I knew my mother was hovering on the other side of the door, casting pretty, troubled glances toward us. I also knew that the quintuplets would soon distract her. I could picture their five heads huddled close to hers in girlish camaraderie. Genteel laughter would fill the room, and everything would grow pleasant and peaceful.

Well, not for long.

I sat in the leather chair across the desk from the prime minister and cleared my throat. I always had a disconnected feeling when I talked to Mr. Sweetwine. His face and voice were so familiar to me from TV and newspapers that I had trouble thinking of him as my stepfather. When my mother first got engaged to him, I used to have these ridiculous fantasies where he and I would discuss current events—you know, I could give him my opinion as a young Canadian who had lived in the real world. I imagined that he would listen thoughtfully and make up his mind about big political decisions based on what I'd said.

Ridiculous.

"I have a suggestion," I said after a moment.

"Splendid." There was a letter on his desk blotter. He

glanced at it, tapped it with one finger, and casually flipped it over to see the return address.

"It's about the quints," I said.

"Oh," he said. "Go on."

"And how you don't want to let them go into the real world."

He looked at me. He seemed to be listening to me, but I could tell he was far away.

"If you want to read that letter first, I don't mind," I said.

"What letter?"

He was holding it between his thumb and forefinger. I stared at it.

"Oh," he said with a hearty chuckle. "Not at all. What were you saying?"

"If the quintuplets are ever going out in the real world," I said, "they'll have to learn more than they're learning in school."

"Really."

"Yes." I fixed him with a hard look. "They'll need to learn how to ride a bus, shop for groceries, stuff like that."

"Not necessary," he said. "The quintuplets are well-provided for. There is little danger of them ever having to ride buses or buy groceries."

"You mean when they become ambassadors of good will."

He looked pleased in a vague sort of way. "Is that what they told you?"

"Yes," I said. "What *is* that, exactly?"

"I expect they want to bring comfort and support to those in need," he said, "throughout the world."

I stared at him.

"The girls will develop a knowledge of world affairs," he said. "They will represent our country's concerns regarding crucial issues."

"How are they going to do that," I asked, "if they can't even go to the store by themselves?"

He'd forgotten about the letter. He sat back in his chair and scratched his ear. "You're saying they need a more practical side to their education," he said.

"Yes!"

"How?"

"If you won't let them off the grounds—" I said.

"Absolutely not. Not after that unmitigated—"

"Then let us do it here. We can think of stuff from real life and practise it here, almost like Games. It's not perfect, but it's better than what we learn sitting in that classroom."

He put his fingers together in a little steeple and rested his chin on them. "I've been assured that the education my daughters receive in that classroom is the best in the world."

"But in the real world, kids learn stuff *outside* the school, too. We go on field trips, join sports, belong to clubs, and stuff."

Mr. Sweetwine frowned.

"It's an odd idea," he said.

"I guess it seems like it to you," I said, "but I bet if you asked my mother, she'd say yes. I bet if you asked her opinion as a psychologist."

His face softened as I talked about my mother. He practically smiled at me.

"If you were to try this Games thing," he said, "just as an experiment, how would you begin?"

I drew a deep breath and smiled back at him. "This is what I think," I said, and leaned forward to explain it.

🍁 🍁 🍁

Twenty minutes later, I was in Gummy's sitting room with a clipboard and a stub of pencil. Nanny Grayson, who had settled crosswise in the big chair with a fashion magazine in one hand and her bare feet dangling, shot me a wary look, shrugged, and flipped a page.

"We'll need some gauzy stuff for turbans, a couple of suitcases, and one of those foreign-language phrase books," I said. "Can you help us out?"

Mrs. Gummidge exchanged a superior look with Nanny Grayson, but curiosity got the better of them.

"Going on a trip?" asked Nanny Grayson.

"I should be so lucky," I answered. "Do you have any foreign money?"

"From which country?"

"India, if you have it. Otherwise, any old place. And Gummy, can you whip up some tandoori chicken and chapatis for dinner tomorrow?"

Mrs. G. floundered. She seemed torn between the sudden

request for foreign foods and the fact that I'd called her Gummy again.

"Does this have something to do with your meeting with Mr. Sweetwine?" inquired Nanny Grayson.

I lowered the clipboard, sighed, and nodded. I frowned. "I guess it wouldn't be nice to accuse someone of running his country better than he runs his family."

"Not nice *at all,*" Mrs. Gummidge agreed. She would have gone on, but Wilton Amaryllis—he's the gardener, as I may have mentioned—poked his head into the cook's sitting room. As usual, he held his cat Fluffy under one arm. Any self-respecting cat would have hissed and scratched to get away, but that fat old feline just hung there, purring.

"Willa had a special meeting with Mr. Sweetwine after dinner," explained Nanny Grayson, "and she was just going to tell us what it was all about."

"Oh," said Wilton in a bored way.

"What it's about," I said, "is Games."

"Oh . . . games. I see," said Wilton.

"And the foreign currency and the suitcase and so on?" prompted Nanny Grayson.

"Immigration rights," I said. "We're going to investigate issues by making up games about them. We're going to do some hands-on scenarios and the first one is 'Immigration Rights.'"

"The *first* one? . . ." Mrs. Gummidge repeated.

I got the impression that Wilton Amaryllis had forgotten what he'd come for. He stared at me with his jaw a little slack, like someone watching a rerun of an old movie. Fluffy squinted, lifted her head adoringly toward him, and purred louder.

"Yes, Mr. Sweetwine was totally in favor of the idea after I explained it," I said.

"You explained it?"

"He says Games closely approximate the realities of modern life and stimulate interest in world affairs, allowing young minds to expand in an environment of trial and error."

"He said that?" echoed Nanny Grayson.

"He says the ancient Greeks had Games, and look what happened to *them.*"

Nanny Grayson stole a glance at the others.

"So how about those chapatis, Gummy?" I finished up. "Can you throw something together?"

"It has always been a mystery to *me,*" she exploded, "how the children in this house are unable to pronounce my full *name,* when at the age of *four* they could say 'opposition leader' and 'filibuster.' . . . Don't *you* start." This last bit was aimed at Nanny Grayson, who was trying not to laugh.

"Furthermore," continued Mrs. Gummidge, "we do not 'throw things together' when we dine in this house. You might as well accuse Wilton Amaryllis of planting artificial flowers."

He snorted. Mrs. Gummidge went on, "I have never 'whipped up' a meal—least of all an *ethnic* one—and I don't intend to start now."

She was finished. She glared.

"Sorry," I said, "I didn't mean it that way." I thought for a long moment and chose my words carefully. "Do you think you could make us some *nan* bread to go with those chapatis? If it wouldn't be too inconvenient, I mean?"

She responded with a cross between a snort and a sob, and the Sweetwine Games Experiment was on.

🍁 🍁 🍁

"Well, I'm not doing it," said one quint.

Marianne, the one who wore her watch on her right wrist, gasped, "Lianne!"

"Well, I'm not," said Lianne. "Whose idea was this, anyway?"

"Your father wants us to do it," I said. "Anyway, it will be fun. You five don't know enough about fun."

They stared at me with their identical gazes.

"Well, I'm sorry, but it's true. The only thing you know about fun is what the adults tell you, and they don't know anything about it."

"What do you mean?" Lianne was practically yelling. "We have fun. We have a *lot* of fun!"

"Playing checkers and hopscotch," I said. "That's what they told you. They want you to think that's fun."

"It *is* fun!" Lianne bellowed. "You're just trying to get us in trouble!"

I pushed both hands through my hair, making it stand up wildly all over my head. Marianne laughed nervously.

"Look," I said, trying to keep the exasperation out of my voice, "they teach you board games and little songs and jokes because . . . well, they think that's what you're supposed to like, and—"

"Who says we *don't?*" Lianne yelled.

"And it's less trouble for them."

"Less trouble than what?" asked another quintuplet.

"Than normal stuff," I said, "like making up stuff. Trying stuff that might not work. You know. Experimenting."

Five pairs of startled eyes were fixed on me. They really didn't know what I meant.

"We make up things," one of the quintuplets protested.

I raised skeptical eyebrows.

"We made up a play last Christmas," she said. "It was *The Night Before Christmas.*"

"You didn't make it up," I said. "Somebody else wrote it a long time ago."

"We acted it out for the House of Commons Christmas party," said Marianne. "We had a stage downstairs and everything."

"Daddy ordered the costumes from England. Mrs. Gummidge made hot toddies, and Mr. Amaryllis built a real chimney."

"Did you make up any of it by yourselves?" I demanded.

They were puzzled again.

"It was very professional," said Lianne. "Everybody said so."

"But you didn't make it up," I said. "You don't make anything up. I never met kids with less imagination. It's not natural."

"You can't stand there and insult us like that," said Lianne.

But Marianne was frowning. She played with her watchband for a moment. Then she said, "Do other kids . . . do *normal* kids have more imagination than we do?"

There was a sudden silence. All eyes were on me.

"Yes," I said. "They do."

Their faces fell. They exchanged uneasy glances with one another, as if they'd been caught with their blouses untucked.

"That's why we should play this Game," I said. "So we can learn things we don't get to learn in school."

"We make things up? For the Game?" Marianne asked.

"We make it *all* up," I said. "Instead of studying about new Canadians, we'll pretend to be them. We'll imagine what it feels like. We'll get really good at making things up."

They shifted uncomfortably.

"You think other kids are better at making things up than we are?" one of them persisted.

"It comes naturally to most kids," I said. "You just haven't had much practice."

Lianne drew a deep breath and let it out slowly. She looked like someone about to jump out of a plane.

"Okay," she said, "we'll try it."

That was the beginning of the Sweetwine Games Experiment. You've heard of it, I guess. At the outset, it was hotly debated by educators. Also, as you know by now, it ran into a bit of trouble.

But in the beginning, everything went along swimmingly. "Immigration Rights" lasted about two weeks. The adults soon got used to us wearing turbans and veils at the table and asking in foreign languages for butter or salt to be passed. My mother was even mildly amused when we converted the powder room in the lower entryway into a border crossing so we could interrogate dignitaries who came to the official residence on business. You probably read in the newspaper how Paulette Stonewall flatly refused to have her briefcase searched and how Mr. Sweetwine laughed the whole thing off.

Everything was pretty much under control. I was actually enjoying myself for a few minutes each day. And I was so busy thinking about Games that I forgot about Nanny Grayson's midnight wandering. I didn't hear any doors clicking or muffled footsteps or whispered conversations at midnight.

Yes, everything was pretty much under control until the incident about the hair.

Chapter 11

Everyone was surprised when Nanny Grayson had trouble convincing the six of us to come for breakfast. They were all used to that rose-garden life with neat girls working hard at their lessons, sharing mild secrets, and telling harmless jokes. According to Gummy, the quintuplets' daily routine had become a clock by which the rest of the household organized itself. It was a strong undercurrent, a pulse, an irresistible force. So when the children would not come for breakfast, there was a sense of foreboding in the little kingdom.

I heard the whole thing from the top of the stairs, where I was sprawled on the floor with my face pressed between two of the stair rails. I had a clear view of Nanny Grayson's spine, ramrod straight, as she stood in the dining room doorway. Behind her back, she held the note I had shoved under her door just a few minutes earlier.

"Sir, Mrs. Sweetwine," she said, "I'm sorry to disturb you. The children send word that they will not be down for breakfast."

Mr. Sweetwine muttered something unintelligible.

"It's a hunger strike," she explained. "Part of the game they're involved in."

"And the issue is?" rumbled Mr. Sweetwine.

"Immigration rights," said Nanny Grayson. "Specifically, sir, the rights of individuals recently introduced into a . . . um, a country or a community or a . . . well, a family . . . where there are already rules and traditions. . . ."

"The multicultural issue, then? Let's celebrate our differences and so on?"

"Um, yes, sir. Something like that."

"Very well. Tell them to carry on."

"Jordan!" That was my mother. "They *have* to eat breakfast. They really *must*. Miss Grayson, please tell the children to come down this minute or I'll deal with them myself."

Even the quints knew what *that* meant. There were gasps and groans behind me.

"Well," I said unhappily, "I guess we'll have to go down *sometime*. Come on."

Reluctant quintuplets straggled down the stairs behind me. Nanny Grayson, on her way up to fetch us, stopped dead and simply stared. Her mouth dropped open and her eyes bulged.

As we trickled into the dining room, there was a faint yelp from the kitchen. I distinctly heard one of the maids cry, "Oh, Mrs. Gummidge! Oh, you must come! Quick!"

Gummy says the first swing of the door revealed such an improbable scene that it failed to sink in, and she had to wait for the maid's second pass to realize it.

Each of the children in the dining room had a different haircut.

Mr. Sweetwine sat and stared. Nanny Grayson stood behind him looking inscrutable. I was delighted, my mother was practically in tears, and the quintuplets' faces registered everything from guilt to rapture.

"I don't know how it happened," Nanny Grayson gasped. "I was out of the room for about an hour this morning. They were asleep when I checked on them at six o'clock and they were still . . ."

"Unshorn," I supplied.

My mother uttered something like a sob, but I had the distinct impression one of the quints was trying to smother a fit of giggles. I knew right away this was Diane—she had the shortest haircut.

"I'm sorry," said Nanny Grayson.

"You haven't let us down before," said Mr. Sweetwine, "but dammit, Miss Grayson, it's a blow."

"Yes, sir," she said.

I interrupted. "Why are you letting *her* apologize? It wasn't *her* fault."

"Darling, please," said my mother.

"But it wasn't," I persisted. The silence around the table was full of troubled looks. "*I* cut their hair, but I had a good reason." Everyone looked so mournful, I couldn't help laughing. "Not only that, they *enjoyed* it. They *wanted* me to do it. Didn't you?"

The quintuplets stood perfectly still.

"Well, don't be scared. You look *great,* if I do say so myself."

"Willa!" My mother twisted her hands together.

"Young lady . . ." said Mr. Sweetwine.

"You didn't ask permission to give those haircuts," said my mother, "and you knew we wouldn't allow it, so you went behind our backs, didn't you?"

"Furthermore," said Mr. Sweetwine, without waiting for an answer, "you conned the girls into it. They would never try such a thing on their own. Am I right?"

"And I suppose the sink in the quints' bathroom is clogged with hair," added Nanny Grayson.

"Well, I am very sorry about the sink," I admitted.

Mr. Sweetwine lowered his voice and spoke with an awful gentleness which was worse than being yelled at. "You fail to understand something. Your new stepsisters are not ordinary little girls. They have a special life, a special mission. They are the darlings of an entire nation, and decisions about them are *special* decisions, not to be made by a child with a pair of kitchen shears."

The whole room held its breath while I met his terrible gaze for several seconds. The maid was actually trembling as she collected the plates.

"Bull-whackey," I said at last. "Sir."

He was shocked beyond speech.

"Willa!" my mother exploded.

A quintuplet—it was Anne, the one with the page-boy haircut—began to laugh uncontrollably and had to be sent from the room.

"You haven't even asked me why I did it," I pointed out in my most reasonable voice.

Mr. Sweetwine's face was as red as a geranium. He said, "I'm sure you had the noblest of motives, but right now I don't wish to hear them. You'd better go to your room."

I stared. I curled my fingers so tightly they ached. My hands were like two hard knots. My voice cracked. "In this house, out of all the houses in the country . . . I thought there would be room for discussion. New ideas, you know?" I was shaking so hard I had to stop for breath.

My mother picked up her coffee cup, set it down again, and covered her mouth with an unsteady hand. Mr. Sweetwine riveted his eyes on the view through the window.

"But when it comes to those quintuplets, you're blind. Just plain stinking blind!"

I stomped from the room, slamming the French doors behind me.

The remaining quintuplets followed me from the dining room in a flurry of braids, headbands, and flowing tresses.

🍁 🍁 🍁

Mr. Sweetwine stood in the doorway of my bedroom. My mother was with him. Beyond them, I caught a glimpse of Nanny Grayson as she slipped into the quintuplets' room. It reminded me of the times I had seen her moving silently through the corridor after dark, and I wondered what would happen if I brought up those incidents now. It would probably have the desired effect of distracting my mother—so much so that she would be sure to dismiss it as a lie. Not only that, it would make her angrier than ever. I kept my mouth shut.

The twitter of quintuplet voices rose and fell until Nanny Grayson shut the door. It gave a quiet click which made me, in spite of everything else, shudder.

"Discussion," said my stepfather.

I studied the clean white paint of the windowsill.

"Would you please," he asked patiently, "explain why you cut the quintuplets' hair?"

I said, "Because I couldn't tell them apart."

"What!"

"What!" repeated my mother.

I stumbled on. "And because you won't let me go home."

Mr. Sweetwine spoke through gritted teeth. "I don't quite see what one has to do with the other."

"I used to have a pretty normal life," I said, "but coming here is like going to *prison*. I can't go to my old school or go to the mall or do anything *normal* anymore."

He looked at my mother. She nodded slowly and sat on the edge of my bed.

"She could invite a friend over," he mused out loud. "We could run a security check on the family."

"That's not what I meant!" I burst out. "It's like . . . I mean, I have five new sisters and I can't even tell them apart! Except Marianne, I mean. Sometimes." It was getting harder and harder to say exactly what I meant.

"Don't you *like* your new sisters?" asked my mother.

"Sure. I guess."

"If you liked them," argued Mr. Sweetwine, "you wouldn't have done this to them."

"I didn't *do* anything to them! They *wanted* those haircuts!"

This failed to make much of an impression on him. He drew calming breaths and only half-listened. My mother smoothed the bedspread with her hand.

"You talked them into it," she said.

"They would have asked permission a long time ago if they weren't so scared of you."

The prime minister fixed me with the glare that had squelched three heads of state and a United Nations task force. "My own daughters are not afraid of me," he growled.

"Some of them are. Suzanne is," I countered. "Marianne is, a bit." At the look on his face, I hurried to add, "But I think they're a little better these days. Since the wedding. I'm almost sure."

Mr. Sweetwine slumped.

"Jordan," said my mother. "What if . . . I mean, we could trim them all as short as . . ." She gestured helplessly at her own neat hair.

"Diane," I said.

"And then they would all look the same again," Mr. Sweetwine finished.

"Well, yes," said my mother.

"Wait!" I cried. "How will I know which one is which?"

"You!" My mother was still furious. "You think an entire country should suffer just because you want to be able to tell your sisters apart?"

I shook my head wearily. "I just want things to be normal. That's all. Just ordinary. If you won't let me go back to Dad . . ."

My mother made a choking sound and sat back as if she'd been slapped. I broke off in midsentence and felt the hot blood rush into my face. "I never meant . . . I . . . I'm sorry."

"Darling," she said in a strangled voice. "You don't realize how much that hurts me."

"I'm sorry," I said again.

"Of course, this is a difficult time of adjustment for you," said Mr. Sweetwine. "We understand that. But *you* must understand that the whole country is watching this family. We . . . your mother and I . . . must project a certain image. Can't you try to get along here for a few months? You know what happened the last time we tried to arrange a visit."

"For Pete's sake," I said. "I *told* you—it was just a little welcoming committee. That's what I mean. The way we live here is so . . . so smothering! If things were more normal . . ."

I stole a glance at my mother. I could feel the heat flushing high in my cheeks. She looked so unhappy that I glanced away again and added weakly, "At least, if I could tell the quints apart . . ."

Mr. Sweetwine rubbed his eyes, dragged one hand over his face, and sighed heavily.

"You drive a hard bargain," he said.

"Yes."

He let out a hollow laugh, tapped a short rhythm on my dresser, and rubbed his face. "All right. We'll tidy up those haircuts and leave them as they are. For now."

"Jordan," protested my mother.

"For a while," he insisted. "Maybe the press will love it. We'll see how it affects the opinion polls." He ran his fingers through his hair. "Now, I've got a summit meeting, and it can't be more work than this *breakfast* has been."

I pulled a face, which made him stop on his way out to add, "One thing, miss. If you ever say *bull-whackey* to me again . . . Do you take my meaning? People conducting a serious discussion do not use expressions like *bull-whackey.*"

"Actually," I said, "that's sort of hard to believe. Sir."

He shook his head. "I'm not speaking now as your prime minister," he said. "I'm speaking as your stepfather."

After this conversation, according to Mrs. Gummidge, my mother returned to the dining room. She was clearly in need of a little bracing. Gummy poured her another cup of coffee and closed the door gently, leaving my mother to contemplate the terrible prospect of suddenly having six daughters, all different.

Chapter 12

Mrs. Gummidge's strong hands plunged into the grocery bags and dragged out roasts of beef, bunches of carrots, and sacks of flour. As each item emerged, she slapped it on the big kitchen table, as if rough treatment would help to transform the ingredients into a tender and delicious meal. I watched her plunk down a chicken, a couple of large turnips, and a box of salt. When she snatched up the eggs, I braced myself for the crunch and splat, but she cradled the carton like a newborn in the crook of her arm and shoved her other hand deep into the sack.

I was folding paper bags. There were dozens of them. The kitchen staff, who had transferred the supplies out of the delivery van, were busy in the pantry, shifting things around and ticking them off their checklists. I could hear them laughing and joking as they worked.

"Tomato juice," grunted Mrs. Gummidge, banging it on the table. "Green onions. More green onions. Bacon."

"I was wondering," I said, smoothing the crease out of a bag with the flat of my hand.

She stopped in midthump with a wary look in her eyes.

"I was wondering," I repeated more boldly, "whether there's ever been any trouble here. At night."

"Trouble?" she echoed. "What kind of trouble?"

Her expression was less than inviting. Not what you would call friendly, open, or encouraging. She held a package of coffee in one solid fist.

"Um," I said, "people creeping through the halls after midnight, for example. Acting suspiciously. Disappearing through doors. Things like that."

"What on *earth* have you been reading?" she demanded, slashing open the foil packet and dumping the coffee into a cannister. "Does your mother know you read those kinds of books?"

"I'm serious," I said.

The wary look came back into her face. She slapped the lid on the cannister, screwed it more tightly than necessary, and grunted.

"At night," I repeated patiently. "Do people ever sneak around this house?"

"Certainly not," she said. "The guard on duty would never allow it."

"But," I persisted, "if one of the people creeping around *was* a guard . . ."

She dropped the bag of potatoes she'd been manhandling. They rolled all over the table. When she sank onto the kitchen stool, I thought for a wild moment that she might burst into tears. Her face changed completely. The lines on her jowls slackened. Her cheeks went flabby and hollow.

"What do you mean?" she asked in a thin voice. For someone who had been punishing groceries, she sounded awfully feeble. The abrupt change in her manner startled me so much that I began to fumble for words.

"For example," I said, wondering at her wide scared eyes. "If I accidentally heard something about blackmail."

"Blackmail?" she echoed. *"You* know who the blackmailer is?" She pursed her lips and gave me a skeptical look. "Who is it, then?"

I stopped folding bags. I stood with my hands flat on the table, waiting for her to go on. But she didn't.

"So you're saying there really is a blackmailer?" I persisted. "Somebody really is being blackmailed? Someone in this house?"

"Certainly not," she said, but her attempt to cover up was pathetic, and she could see I knew it immediately. She peered at me from beneath her fierce eyebrows. "Good heavens, what have I said? Come here, now. Come!"

Her strong hand closed around my wrist. I let out a squawk.

"Don't be so melodramatic," she scolded, dragging me down the hall to her sitting room, where she slammed the door.

"Now," she commanded. "You are to tell me everything. Everything. *Who* did you hear? *When? Where* were they? And *what* exactly did they say?"

This abrupt change from cranky-and-frightened Gummy to towering-and-majestic Mrs. Gummidge startled me badly. I sucked in a shivering breath, looked straight into her pink face, and said, "It's Nanny. She's up to no good."

She goggled. She was furious. She curled her big fists tight like two rocks. She loomed over me like the wall of a medieval fortress.

"Is that who you've been eavesdropping on? Is that who you've seen in the halls at night?"

"Well," I said.

"And who was she speaking to? Tell me that."

I shrugged, but there was no stopping her now.

"Nick Andrews," she said crisply.

I gasped.

"Oh, good heavens, Willa. You've got the whole thing entirely backward."

She was on her feet. "I'll tell you this *once,* and *once* only, so you listen to me," she said. "You leave Nanny and Nick alone. I mean it."

"But what if they're blackmailing somebody? What if they're the ones who told the newspaper about my father's letter?"

"They are *not,* you foolish child. They have nothing to do with it." She snatched one of the cushions from the couch and plumped it so vigorously I was afraid it would explode. "I don't know where you get such ridiculous ideas."

I got them from her. I thought she would have figured that out by now. I tried to shoot her a reproachful look, but she was busy pounding cushions and slamming them back onto the sofa.

"I'll not say one more word about this," she said. "You listen to me. You hear?"

"But the blackmailers . . ."

"There is no such thing," she said.

"But you *said* so!"

"I didn't. *You're* the one who used that ridiculous word.

72

Obviously, you're imagining things. I've never known a child to overreact in this appalling manner. You'll be the death of me."

She hammered the last cushion against the arm of the chair, dusted her hands, and looked down at me with a perfectly Gummy-ish glance.

"Have you finished folding those bags, then?" she asked, and the only thing left to do was to follow her back to the kitchen.

Chapter 13

My father began to send postcards. The first batch arrived just before breakfast. Mr. Sweetwine started to yell as soon as he saw them—he was developing fast reflexes when it came to the Howard Problem.

If I hadn't been so engrossed in chapter fourteen of *The Happy Dooleys on Location,* I would have heard the ruckus sooner, but I was flat on my stomach behind my unmade bed, lost in the scene where Lucinda invites the spoiled child actor to join the Dooleys for dinner, making him realize the value of a wholesome meal and a loving family. Lucinda had just dished him up some mashed potatoes when it dawned on me that Mr. Sweetwine's voice was trumpeting through the household.

I scurried down the stairs to the dining room, where the quintuplets sat staring at their father with owlish eyes.

"A hundred and twenty!" Mr. Sweetwine was shouting. "A hundred and *twenty!* What's wrong with the man?"

Marianne chewed the collar of her sweatshirt. She looked as if she might start crying or laughing uncontrollably.

"Who is he talking about?" I whispered.

"Your father," she whispered back.

Mr. Sweetwine's hands were full of postcards. There were postcards on the table and on the floor. They fluttered as he waved his hands.

"What did he do?" he roared. "Run them off on a *Xerox?*"

"I don't think that would work," I pointed out helpfully. "Something that stiff would get jammed in the machine."

He turned on me. His eyes were wild. His hair stuck up all over his head. I almost felt sorry for him.

"A hundred and twenty!" he thundered.

"Jordan!" cried my mother. "You're frightening the children."

We weren't frightened. Actually, the quints reminded me more of spectators at a tennis match. Their faces were bright and interested. Nevertheless, my new stepfather drew a deep breath, shoved one hand through his hair, and spoke in a soft strained voice. "He's handwritten every blessed one of these cards. It must have taken him all day."

"You know how he gets," said my mother. "He's a bit intense."

The question was pushing up inside me. I couldn't keep it down. "What did he write?"

My mother glared. Mr. Sweetwine looked like someone who had swallowed a hard-boiled egg in one gulp. He pressed one hand to his heart like a swooning lover and read in a sarcastic voice, "My *darling* Louise. *Please* come *back* to me."

It is hard to describe the volcano that boiled up inside me when he did this. The trembling started in the pit of my stomach. My fingers curled into knots and my blood grew hot.

"Jordan, I'm sorry," said my mother in a helpless voice.

He whirled on her. "Don't *you* apologize! It's not *your* fault you married a lunatic!"

One of the quintuplets giggled. He turned sharply on her.

"I'm talking about her *first* husband," he barked. "He's a raving madman. I ought to have him locked up!"

He knew instantly he had gone too far with this. My mother, who had been all soft and apologetic a moment ago, rose to her feet. She stared him down. After a minute, he had to look away.

"It's just," he said in a tight voice, "that I can't stand the crazy things he does to try to get you back."

"I know," she said. "But you and I are married now." She put her hand on his arm and nodded him toward the door. "It's a big change for all of us. It might take him a little while to accept it, but he will. Believe me."

They stopped right in front of me, where she fixed me with a searching look. "And he *is* still your dad, isn't he, darling?" She put one cool hand on the side of my face. "Have a good breakfast," she said as she left with Mr. Sweetwine.

I broke open like a dropped egg. I was shocked to find myself sitting at the breakfast table with my face on my arms, sobbing into a pile of postcards while the quintuplets fluttered around me like moths. A storm of hands patted my back and my hair. The quints murmured comforting things and whispered to one another. When Mrs. Gummidge arrived with the breakfast, she clucked at me.

"Now, then," she said. "You girls take your sister right upstairs and let her wash her face. She'll feel better after that good cry, won't you, lovey?" She patted me as if I were a loaf of new bread. "It's boiled eggs and toast, and naturally it won't keep, and I'll have to do breakfast all over again, but that's all right. It's awfully hard on you, all this, isn't it? Off you go, now. Your sisters will look after you."

Upstairs, I washed my face. The quints scooted around like a chorus of ballet dancers circling a dying swan. I had to lie down and pretend to be asleep to get them to go away. Then, when they were gone, I really did fall asleep.

🍁 🍁 🍁

It felt strange to wake up in the quintuplets' room. I lay there for a long time, studying the way the sunlight bounced across the ceiling and wondering what it would be like to share a room with the five of them. After I demanded my own room, no one had taken away the extra bed in the quints' room—the bed that had been meant for me. I wondered which one it was. I could hear a motorboat on the river and the voices of quintuplets in the hall below me. There was a smell of coffee in the air.

I still clutched one of my father's postcards. The picture was the same as the others I'd seen in the dining room—a clock made of flowers, with the words *Westmount* and *Tempus Fugit* set out in sweet alyssum. I remembered the day my father had bought the boxes of postcards—thousands of them—for fifteen dollars at the city auction. I remembered helping him carry them out to his shed, and how he'd laughed when I asked why he wanted them. He hadn't answered. I didn't care. I loved it when he laughed.

My hand was chilly and awkward from sleeping. I turned the card over.

MY DARLING LOUISE
PLEASE COME BACK TO ME. I LOVE YOU.
HOWARD XOXOXOXOXOX

Tears burned my eyes, but I forced them back and lay still, staring at the ceiling through the blur. I thought hard for a long time. Then I got up and washed my face, shoved the postcard in my pocket, and went downstairs.

🍁 🍁 🍁

Mrs. Gummidge gave me some warm muffins, an orange, and a glass of milk. I ate them at the table in her sitting room while the kitchen staff cleaned up the breakfast mess in the kitchen. It was peaceful in Gummy's room. No one bothered me. I opened my notebook and wrote *Dear Dad* at the top of the first page. The letter was so long I didn't finish it until lunchtime.

Mrs. Gummidge appeared in the doorway. She wore her purple cardigan. She carried a wooden spoon like a flag, cupping one hand underneath it to catch the drips. The spoon was covered in tomato sauce as thick and red as blood.

I glared at her. She glared back at me.

"She ought to get back together with my father," I said. "She's not happy here. It's so obvious. She doesn't even know what's good for her."

Mrs. Gummidge studied me. As I closed my notebook, I could feel her fiery gaze on the top of my head.

"I see," she said. "You've got it figured out, have you? Your mother should divorce Mr. Sweetwine and remarry your father, and then she would be happy."

I hesitated. If I'd had a script, I'd have been fumbling through the pages, looking for my lines.

"You just said . . ." she prompted.

"Never mind."

"Do you realize," she went on, "that most of the evil in this world is done by people who think they know what's best for other people? I'd have thought *you* had more sense."

I scowled at her. "What's *that* supposed to mean?" My cheeks felt as hot and red as the tomato sauce on her spoon.

"I was thinking," she said, "how furious you get when people try to tell *you* what's best."

"That's different!" I yelled.

She sniffed and shook her head. When I didn't go on, she started to go away. Then she stopped. "You might consider," she said, "how upsetting this is for your mother."

"My father loves her!" I said in a low furious voice. "He wants her back! He only wants the best thing for her!"

"And of course that's all *you're* thinking of—what's best for your mother."

"You're trying to make me take sides!" I shoved my plate across the table so hard that my orange peels tumbled to the floor. "This is not my fault, you know! Why does everybody think this is my fault?"

She pointed the spoon at me.

"Nobody thinks that." She hitched her cardigan up around her throat as she started back toward the kitchen. "As far as I can tell, nobody in this house thinks that. And you'll be kind enough to pick up those peels, won't you? Thank you very much."

After lunch, the quints and I did some research on "Endangered Species," which was the game of the week after "Immigration Rights" and which, unfortunately, led to some trouble. For one thing, we weren't able to find any endangered species on the grounds of the official residence. Marianne was especially sorry that there were no eastern cougars to protect, a fact that she mentioned two or three times a day. For another, we'd been preparing picket signs and banners for an endangered species rally, but it wasn't going to be much fun without an audience. The household staff was already sick of listening to us and had started to make jokes and rude comments about our posters and petitions.

Then, of course, there was the incident with Nanny Grayson.

I was alone in the playroom on the second floor when I saw her. It's incredible what can happen in your mind when you pretend even for an hour or two to be an endangered animal. At least, that's the only way I can explain what happened.

Ever since lunchtime, I had been prowling the quints' second floor playroom, delving deep into my animal instincts so I could play the role of the eastern wolverine. I was trying hard to get into the part. I willed myself to be ferocious and insatiable. I imagined for myself a pair of strong jaws, which could crunch huge bones and rip open frozen meat. I knew how many hundreds of kilometers I roamed in search of food each day, and I knew exactly how it felt to be confined to a wildlife refuge by well-meaning humans.

When you think about it, you'll realize this was the worst possible time for Nanny to slip past the playroom.

I suppose she thought the room was empty. She probably thought I was downstairs with the quints, writing letters to the Canadian Wildlife Service. She did not expect the playroom to be inhabited by that fiercest and most ruthless of creatures, *Gulo gulo,* the eastern wolverine. As soon as she slipped past, I scurried to the playroom door and peered at her with the silent gaze of a vicious predator. From behind, she seemed almost innocent, hurrying along with her red cardigan flapping against the sides of her skirt in a businesslike way. She did not plan to encounter a *Gulo gulo*—especially one that had been watching her clandestine movements, secret meetings, and mysterious conversations for the past few weeks.

As you may know, there is nothing more dangerous than a *Gulo gulo* that has been thwarted. And I, who had tried to expose the enemy's evil deeds to Mrs. Gummidge and had been *brushed off,* had been magnificently thwarted.

As if that weren't enough, Nanny Grayson was moving nervously down the corridor, peeking over her shoulder, placing her hand on the doorknob of *my* room.

The *Gulo gulo* will do almost anything to defend its territory. Not that I considered the quiet room my territory, not exactly. I preferred to think of it as a temporary place and felt about it the way Lucinda Dooley felt about the bedroom in Hollywood where she spent most of her time longing to go home. But when Nanny Grayson slipped into my room I was suddenly furious.

I know what they mean by "the heat of the moment." My ears grew hot. My eyes burned. A flush warmed my face from my powerful jaws to the hair that prickled along my spine.

By the time I reached the doorway and, clinging to the jamb, peered around it into the blue bedroom, the enemy was making soft rustling noises, rummaging through my things.

Blood really does boil. It creates a bubbling sensation in the *Gulo gulo*'s stomach and sends fire into the veins.

I shoved the door as wide open as it would go. It crashed against the dresser, and I hurled myself into the room.

"What are you doing?" I yelled.

She could not have been more startled. She jumped, and when she whirled to face me, she was feverish and her eyes were huge and bright as if she might burst out crying.

It was bad enough to find her searching through my things. It was worse to realize she'd seen, and maybe read, the letter to my father, which was on my desk. But worst of all, she was standing on the far side of the bed with some folded pink pages in one hand and *The Happy Dooleys on Location* in the other.

"What is the meaning of this?" she demanded in a trembling voice.

"What?" I hollered.

"I knew you were high-spirited," she said. Her voice broke. "I knew you were independent. But I honestly didn't realize you were . . . so . . . sly."

I didn't understand. I stared at her. I could think about nothing except the *Happy Dooley* book and how I'd left it there on the floor when Mr. Sweetwine began shouting this morning and how strange it seemed that Nanny Grayson was so furious with me for reading it.

"It's not that bad," I protested.

She flung the book on the bed and waved the pink pages at me. "How *dare* you make light of this? This is my *private* correspondence, and you had no right to go in my room and take it! Who do you think you are?"

I had a sudden crazy urge to burst into tears. It infuriated me. I choked it back and yelled, "I didn't! I don't know what you're talking about!"

She stopped and glared at me. Her face was red. She pulled her mouth into a tight knot of rage.

"I think you do," she said. "Someone saw you sneak into my room this morning and come out with this letter in your hand."

"I *didn't!*" I stared at the letter, which was on the same pink paper I had seen . . . somewhere . . . before. I squinted at it and tried to remember, but Nanny bulldozed the thoughts right out of my head, saying, "Willa, here it is. Right here. How do you explain that?"

The tears came. It was horrible. I was sobbing and trying to shout at the same time, stumbling stupidly over my words. "The quints! They hate me! They're . . . playing a trick on me and it's not fair! Everybody hates me!"

"Stop it," she said.

"I *didn't* do anything! I *didn't!*"

"All right," she said.

My face was hot and slick with tears, and the sobs came in great spasms, making me cough in an ugly voice.

"That's enough," she said.

"What's wrong?" It was a quintuplet, innocent and gracious as ever. I jerked my head out of my hands and saw a blurry Marianne standing in the doorway.

"You *did* this," I raged. "It's not funny!"

"What?"

"Willa," said Nanny. "You don't really believe the quints would do something like this, do you?"

"Something like what?" Marianne asked.

"They *hate* me!" I cried.

"We do not," Marianne protested.

"We'll say no more about it," Nanny said, "but I never want such a thing to happen again. Is that understood?"

"I didn't *do*—"

"Fine. I know you're going through a hard time right now. I just want you to know that unacceptable behavior is unacceptable behavior, no matter what."

"I'm going to tell my mother," I sobbed.

Nanny hesitated.

"Tell her what?" echoed Marianne.

"If you want to upset your mother more than she already is," said Nanny, "that's your choice. In my opinion you'd just be making a bad situation worse." She tucked the letter into the pocket of her red sweater and stood watching me for a long moment. When I didn't say anything more, she came around the end of the bed, slipped past Marianne and me, and disappeared into the corridor.

I gave way to a fresh storm of tears and flung myself onto the bed.

"What happened?" Marianne persisted, sitting beside me.

"Someone's trying to get me in trouble!" I wailed and cried harder.

"Not me," she said simply.

After a moment, she went away and came back with a roll of toilet paper.

"Here," she said.

I blew my nose noisily and drew a shuddering breath. When I emerged from behind the handful of tissue, she was holding the *Happy Dooley* book in both hands, studying it.

"Is this good?" she asked.

I resisted a terrible urge to yank it from her hands and squirrel it away in its hiding place.

"You like this?" she persisted.

"Not really," I said.

"It looks like an old book," she said.

My heart was flying around like a crow in a woodshed, beating hard, struggling to escape.

"It's trash," I said, reaching for the book. "Outdated. *Terrible* role models."

"Can I read it?" she asked.

"Better not," I said.

"Why?"

"It's bad for you. My mother said so."

She looked at it wistfully. Lucinda Dooley grinned up at her from the faded green cover. A ring of coffee stained Lucinda's neck, dangling there like a giant earring.

"I don't think so," Marianne argued. "If you don't like it, can't I just read it for a while?"

I was afraid to say no. I was afraid Marianne would go to my mother with those big innocent eyes and start asking questions about the Happy Dooleys. I shrugged. I made a careless sound and drew another shuddering breath, still recovering from so much crying. I was exhausted and desperate. There wasn't a flicker of the *Gulo gulo* left in me.

"I'll give it back when I'm done," Marianne promised. "Come downstairs?"

"In a minute," I replied, as though I had better things to do, and she left, taking the *Happy Dooley* book with her.

Chapter 14

I didn't mean to eavesdrop. I mean, I didn't plan it. I was just sitting there on the porch step in the darkness when my mother stomped into the sunroom, whirled to face Wilton Amaryllis, who had shuffled in behind her, and said, "Mr. Amaryllis, when I ask you to make a change to the garden I expect you to carry out my wishes immediately, do you hear me?"

You have to admit it: This was not the time to stand up, clear my throat, and say brightly, "Oops. Excuse me. I'm just passing through."

I hunkered down on the step with my back to them and listened.

"Them lilies have been in that spot for twelve years," Wilton argued back. "Mrs. Sweetwine . . . I'm talking about the first Mrs. Sweetwine . . . she loved them."

"I am not the first Mrs. Sweetwine, am I?" said my mother.

Wilton shifted his weight uncomfortably. I knew how he felt. When my mother uses that tone, it's like being pinned to a corkboard with your wings stretched out.

"If you do not like the way I plan my gardens . . ." Wilton began, and then stopped. He could not seem to think how to finish the sentence.

My mother forced herself to speak more gently. "That has nothing to do with it. I realize that you have taken complete responsibility for the gardens ever since she . . . passed away."

I thought about how the first Mrs. Sweetwine had tumbled headfirst into the Rideau Falls, smashing herself and her expensive camera on the rocks just twelve days after the quints were born. I'm no speechwriter, but I didn't think I would have described this terrible accident as "passing away."

"Yes, ma'am," said Wilton cautiously.

"I admire you for it. I really do."

There was an uncomfortable silence.

"We're all making adjustments to this new marriage, aren't we? We can't expect everything to go smoothly all the time, can we? I understand what you're going through."

He didn't answer. I could imagine him staring past her, studying the reflection of his fierce expression in the dark windows.

"It's just that gardening has always been my special interest," my mother went on. "That's something we have in common, you and I." She was soothing him now. She used to put on that same voice when my father got frustrated about some stink-proof socks he was trying to invent, or some stray-cat detector that kept setting off every car alarm in the neighborhood. I wondered what Wilton would do if she tried to link her arm through his. It was an especially chummy thing she liked to do to someone who was angry with her.

"If we work together—pool our resources, so to speak—I think we can come up with some absolutely breathtaking gardens. What do you say to that?" she coaxed him.

What I would say, if I were Wilton Amaryllis, was that my gardens had always been considered to be plenty breathtaking as they were, and if she didn't like them she could hire herself a garden tractor.

But he didn't.

"Mr. Amaryllis, I want you to know that I am aware that your financial situation is not what it might be, and I—"

"My what?" Wilton interrupted.

"It has come to my attention that you may have some financial concerns at this time, and I want you to rest assured that—"

"Who said so?" he interrupted again.

"I hardly think that's—"

"It's my personal, private business," he said. "And anyone that's been talking around about it ain't necessarily in possession of all the facts. You understand?"

"Yes, but—"

"You don't want to go believing everything you hear about a body. You get my meaning?"

"Mr. Amaryllis!" said my mother in a sharp voice. "I do not go around digging up gossip about members of this household. I am simply trying to alleviate any concerns you might have about the security of your position here."

"That's well and good . . ."

"I'm not finished. I want you to know that I have no plans to carry on here without a gardener. I really don't see how we could manage without you."

"Ma'am, you don't need a gardener. You need a youngster who you can push around—who'll dig where you say and weed when you say. You don't need the likes of me."

"Wait a minute," she said. "Let's not be hasty."

"Nothing hasty about it," he grumbled. "I seen it comin' weeks ago. You might as well fire me now and get it over with."

That annoyed her. I knew it immediately because she turned back into the cool and sophisticated wife of the prime minister. I could almost see her straightening the cuffs of her linen jacket as she said, "As far as I am concerned, and I believe I speak for my husband in this, your position on the household staff is not in question. As long as your work continues to meet the high standards you have always set for yourself, I see no reason why you should go elsewhere."

Wilton thought about that.

"At the same time," said my mother, "I will expect you to carry out my wishes promptly. Beginning with those lily beds."

She probably smoothed a strand of hair back from her lovely cheekbone. I'd seen her do it a million times.

"Do you have any further questions, Mr. Amaryllis?"

He sure didn't. He was upset, but he wasn't crazy. I heard him mutter something. His boots scraped on the tiles as he retreated.

"Good night, then," my mother said. There was nothing irritable about her voice. It floated like a rose petal in the darkness.

Chapter 15

If the quints hadn't been in such a giddy mood when opportunity came knocking, I don't know if they would have come with me. But we were smack in the middle of a rowdy game of "Tag the Endangered Species" when it happened. Lianne, the peregrine falcon, was hiding in trees and on top of garden walls, springing away with a screech every time Suzanne and I, the wildlife conservationists, came into view.

It was very funny. Even Diane, the elusive leatherback turtle, was screaming with laughter.

"Turtle!" I cried, alerting my intrepid partner. We paddled madly across an imaginary ocean, steering our seat cushions down the middle of the sunroom floor with our badminton racket paddles. Diane let us trap her between the wicker loveseat and the door into the garden. We whipped out our collection of snap bracelets, chose a green one, and banded her around the wrist.

She tucked herself into a curled-up ball and rolled under the loveseat.

"What the heck was that?" I demanded.

"I went inside my shell," she explained breathlessly. Suzanne burst out laughing in such an irresistible voice that I began to shriek with laughter, too.

We were still howling and holding our stomachs when Marianne gestured frantically from the cedar hedge at the side of the garden.

"Eastern cougar!" I crowed. Suzanne and I began a mad dash down the yard, waving our snap bracelets and our badminton rackets, still sobbing with laughter. But before we reached Marianne, she pressed one finger to her lips, pointed beyond the hedge, and motioned desperately for us to keep quiet.

On the other side of the hedge, my mother was giving instructions in the firm and pleasant voice usually reserved for television interviews or public lectures.

"We'll need some waterproof tape as well. Do you have some waterproof tape?"

"In the boathouse." That was Wilton Amaryllis's familiar grumble. He sounded, if possible, gloomier than he had last night.

My mother tried to make up for this by speaking in a chirpy manner. "Well, that's fine, then. You can pick it up when you collect the lobster trap."

Wilton shifted his heavy boots, causing little avalanches of dirt and stones. He cleared his throat noisily, as though he were struggling to remember what he wanted to say. Finally, suddenly, he muttered, "There's no call for a lobster trap in that garden."

"I beg your pardon?" My mother had heard him. She just couldn't believe he'd spoken so rudely.

"I ain't never heard of puttin' a lobster trap in a garden," he said. "It ain't done."

Suzanne clapped both hands over her mouth to keep from laughing out loud. Marianne was pink with suppressed mirth.

"Mr. Amaryllis, we went over this matter last night. Now, the plants in this garden have been carefully chosen to represent our Maritime provinces. I intend to reinforce the theme with a decorative lobster trap, and I intend for you to bring it up from the boathouse immediately. Is that clear?"

"Let's go with him." I mouthed the words without speaking, but the other two understood immediately. Their eyes stretched as big as all-season radial tires.

"What?" Marianne mouthed back.

"Come on!"

We retreated to the side of the house, where Lianne had climbed onto the concrete birdbath and was squawking with falconlike laughter.

"We can stow away in his van!" I said breathlessly. "Get a free ride down to the boathouse! Want to?"

Marianne was giggling crazily. "They'll stop us!"

"No, they won't," I whispered back, warming up to the idea,

which had surprised me almost as much as it had surprised them. "I've seen him go in and out a million times. They never check the inside of his van. We can hide in there!"

"You're crazy!" Suzanne hissed, but she was laughing and something sparkled dangerously in her eyes.

"We can do our demonstration," I said. That clinched it. They craned their heads to see Wilton stomping away from the Maritime garden. "But we'll have to hurry."

They hurried, all right. If they hadn't been feeling so wild and powerful and, well, *bad*—they'd never have done it. But it was such a new experience for them to feel free, they'd gotten a bit dizzy with it. They were, I'll admit it, out of control.

Suzanne fled toward the house to collect the equipment for our endangered species project. Marianne and I rounded up the rest of the quints—after finally convincing Lianne to stop flapping and squawking like a falcon—and hustled them into the back of Wilton's van. It wasn't locked. It wasn't even closed. He had been carrying sacks of fertilizer around the side of the house when my mother had started on about the lobster trap, and he had left the van wide open.

I can hardly describe the amount of giggling, snorting, whispering, and shuffling that went on as we hid ourselves. We were almost settled, and Wilton was coming into sight around the hedge, when Suzanne put her hand right on the soft flank of Fluffy the cat, who had gone to sleep in the shadowy van. Fluffy squeaked and growled. Everyone shrieked and snuffled, banging their elbows and sticking their fists in their mouths to stifle hysterical laughter.

I was sure Wilton would notice us, but he didn't. He grumbled and swore under his breath as he crossed the lawn.

There wasn't time to close ourselves in properly before he heaved himself into the driver's seat, slammed the door, and started the engine. After that, we couldn't do it without attracting his attention. So we shoved a gardening glove in the crack to keep the door from closing tight. I had to hang onto the metal crosspiece to prevent the door from bouncing open and shut as we drove.

It was dark inside the van. The tiny scuffles and squeaks of the quintuplets filled the blackness around me, and I hissed, "Shh!"

At the end of the driveway, Wilton slowed and stopped. There was a breath-holding silence.

"Hey, Wilton." That was Nick Andrews, who was on duty at the gate. I strained my ears to hear. "How's things?"

"Don't bother askin'," Wilton growled. "There was plenty to keep me busy before her majesty came bustin' in. Now all's I do is fetch and carry for her. Never seen such foolishness."

"You've got it rough," Nick sympathized.

Wilton muttered something.

"I met that guy Sid up at the police academy," Nick replied, obviously trying to change the subject. "Real hotshot. Top of the class. I heard you put in a good word for him with my boss."

"Yuh," said Wilton.

"You know him, then?"

"Yuh," said Wilton. "Met him a few times."

There was an odd silence.

"No jobs available here, though," Nick said finally. "Not at the moment."

"Yuh," said Wilton. Then he laughed. His voice cracked and scratched as if he hardly ever used it for that purpose. "You guys are hanging on pretty tight to your jobs these days, huh?"

"Mm-hm," said Nick.

Wilton guffawed again. "Yuh. You know a good thing when you got one, eh?"

"Yeah," said Nick. "I guess this Sid guy will have to wait a while if he plans to get a job here."

"I guess so," said Wilton. "Yuh."

A moment later, the van was moving again.

My schemes hardly ever work out as smoothly as this one did. It was as if the quints brought all their tidiness and efficiency with them, even when they were being bad. I never saw anything like it.

The gates clanged shut behind us, the van turned left onto Sussex Drive, and left again down the long winding road to the shore. Within minutes we were crouching in the lilac bushes beside the boathouse, watching Wilton Amaryllis heave the lobster trap into the empty van from which we had tumbled as soon as his back was turned. Among the lilac bushes, I could see the mischievous faces of the quints blinking at me. They seemed more than ever like some new endangered species—

not a shy and elusive species, either, but a quick and playful one.

From our hiding place, we had a brand new view of the official residence. I saw the quints squinting up at it, trying to get used to seeing their kingdom from *outside* the iron fence.

I liked the shore road, which ran for a kilometer between the shore cliffs and the mighty Ottawa River, which had carved them. The road was quiet and unassuming. I had never been on it before, but had looked longingly down at it through the fence at the end of the garden. I liked the way it linked the boathouses, storage buildings, and garages of the embassies and official residences in this privileged neighborhood.

The houses, high on the cliffs, rested safely inside their fences and shared the spectacular scenery. The official residence and the French embassy stood side by side like pleasant strangers, looking out at the wide sweep of river. On the other side of the Sweetwine house was a spooky and beautiful expanse of trees that Gummy called the woodlot, but which I called the mysterious forest. I'd had many imaginary adventures there.

The quints were not having imaginary adventures. This real-life one was exciting enough for them. As soon as Wilton clambered back into the driver's seat and drove off through the mysterious forest on his way back to the house, the quints exploded from the lilac bushes. They jumped and ran and skittered onto the dock, covering their mouths to smother gusts of laughter, grabbing my arms triumphantly, and mussing one another's hair.

It's just a shame that things turned out the way they did.

Chapter 16

I wish I had been there when Wilton Amaryllis burst into the kitchen with a hoe in one hand and a wild look in his eyes, demanding, "Where are they?"

Mrs. Gummidge says she replied, *"Half* the garden you've trekked in, and the *other* half still stuck to that hoe. Get out. Get out this instant!"

"I don't know where they've taken her," he said, "but I'll find them and wring their necks. It's that new one. She puts them up to it. It was never like this before."

"Get out!" said Mrs. Gummidge.

"They've taken my cat!" he wailed. "My Fluffy!"

Mrs. Gummidge says the maid let out a shriek of dismay. Fluffy was a particular favorite of hers. "Oh, terrible!" she cried. "Who? Who took her?"

"It was *them.* Them *five,"* said Wilton. He rapped the hoe on the floor, causing dirt to shower down.

Mrs. Gummidge shouted "Get out!" once more.

"Those five . . ." the maid paused. "Oh, *not* the children!"

"Them *six,"* Wilton corrected himself. "That new one's the ringleader."

"Oh, I don't . . ." the maid was torn. She was fond of the six of us, but she loved Fluffy, too, and now there was a conflict in her loyalties. "Oh, I don't think . . ."

"It were all quiet before she come along," said Wilton.

That's when Nanny Grayson entered the kitchen, saying, "Before *who* came? Has anyone seen the children? They disappeared just before algebra class."

Wilton's face flushed as red as a pomegranate.

"Now, we won't jump to conclusions," advised Mrs. Gummidge.

"Oh," sobbed the maid, clearly having jumped to one.

As Nanny Grayson demanded "What conclusions?" a voice rang out over the grounds.

"NOW HEAR THIS . . . ATTENTION S'IL VOUS PLAÎT . . ."

"Whatever they've done, it's bilingual," said Nanny Grayson.

The four adults tumbled over the kitchen step into the yard.

"COULD I HAVE YOUR ATTENTION, PLEASE? VOTRE ATTENTION, S'IL VOUS PLAÎT."

Mrs. Gummidge says it seemed as if everything within five kilometers held its breath. Birds stopped singing. The pleasure boats on the river seemed to pause. My mother, who was gathering roses from the west garden, stopped and shaded her eyes.

"WE WOULD LIKE TO DRAW YOUR ATTENTION TO A SERIOUS ISSUE—ONE WHICH AFFECTS ALL OF US AND WHICH ONLY WE CAN STOP. WE ARE TALKING ABOUT THE PLIGHT OF ENDANGERED SPECIES: ANIMALS LIKE THE BEAUTIFUL AND ELUSIVE EASTERN COUGAR."

Wilton's "Oh, my God," was echoed by an "Oh, my God," from across the lawn, where my mother had dropped her armful of roses and was pressing both hands to her mouth.

"Oh, my *God,*" squeaked the maid.

"And not a lifejacket among them," Nanny Grayson added morosely.

I have to admit that at the very same moment I was also regretting the lack of lifejackets. It was a pretty big oversight in an otherwise flawless plan. Wilton's old rowboat with the five horsepower motor was slow and tippy. All five quints were sitting down—two in the bow and three in the stern—but I was standing amidships feeling a bit wobbly, and the quints were waving their placards more energetically than I would have liked. Also, we were farther from shore than I had intended. The boathouse looked as small as a loaf of bread, and the people watching us through the fence were as tiny as crumbs. Still, there we were. I clutched the squirming bundle under my arm, raised the microphone again, and cleared my throat. The sound boomed across the open water.

"VOTRE ATTENTION, S'IL VOUS PLAÎT."

By this time, Nick Andrews and two other security guards had rounded the side of the house and stopped dead, staring. I repeated the message about the eastern cougar in French, but before I could finish, two things happened. The bundle under my arm began to wiggle frantically, and my mother shrieked "Willa! What are you doing?"

This was an ill-timed query. Her voice froze me and electrified the wriggling cat, which twisted, howled, and scrambled out of the towel I'd wrapped around her. She was full of static electricity and unholy fury. With a slither and a leap, she landed on my shoulder, then tried to clamber onto my head.

The boat rocked wildly. Three placards spun overboard. The quintuplets clutched at the gunwales. Marianne screamed.

On the shore, there were answering screams. My mother and Mrs. Gummidge ran forward, but stopped abruptly at the edge of the lawn. They were high above us, locked inside the iron fence above the steep twisting terrace steps. In any case, we were too far out on the river for anyone to reach us without a boat.

According to Mrs. Gummidge, Nanny Grayson was saying, "I'll kill them. As soon as I get my hands on them, I'll kill them."

"Willa! Sit down this instant!" shouted my mother. "Bring back that boat right now! Where are your lifejackets? What do you think you're doing?"

I was too busy to respond to this barrage of parental concern. Fluffy had gained the summit, and for a few precarious seconds she managed to balance on top of my head. Maybe she liked the view from up there, maybe she thought the shore was closer than it was, or maybe all her seagoing urges abruptly deserted her. In any case, she was suddenly airborne with her claws spread and her mouth wide open.

Everyone shrieked. The boat kicked and bucked, and I fell to my knees.

Fluffy hit the water in a fine cat version of a bellyflop, complete with sprawling limbs and a look of utter surprise. The boat continued to rock. I tried to get up, but tripped over a placard. At the same time, four of the five quintuplets grabbed for Fluffy.

It was the sudden lunge cat-ward that did us in.

"They're going over!" screamed my mother.

Water poured over the gunwale, the boat tipped, and all six

of us spilled into the river, as Gummy says, like peaches out of a jar.

"Oh! Oh!" gasped the maid.

"Fluffy!" shouted Wilton.

Nick and the other guards finally managed to unlock the iron gate and turn off all the alarms, and everybody raced down the six flights of twisting steps to the shore road.

"Hang onto the boat!" I was shouting in a watery voice. "Hey! Suzanne! Hang onto the boat!"

The boat was upside down, drifting east with the current. For a moment I saw only three heads bobbing, then there seemed to be eight. There was so much movement I couldn't count them.

But something else was happening. The motorboats and dinghies and sailboats and tour boats that had been lazing along the river began to converge on our overturned rowboat. As they drew nearer you could hear people calling to us and to one another: "Hang onto the boat! We'll be right there! . . . Hey, it's the quintuplets! It's the Sweetwine quintuplets!"

It turned into a sensation. All across the water you could hear the word *quintuplets* like an echo. Quints were being fished out left and right—I couldn't tell how many. Strong hands grabbed me from behind and dragged me straight out of the water onto the deck of a sailboat. People pumped my hand and thumped my back in a congratulatory way. From my new vantage point I could see more of the action. Boats that had shown no interest in rescuing six ordinary children began to turn and close in on us, hoping for a glimpse of the famous Sweetwine quintuplets.

"Hey! Hey!" I could see Nick and the other security guards shouting from the foot of the steep terrace, but the excited chatter of people on the rescue boats drowned them out. We were in a cluster of vessels that grew more crowded by the minute. Already it looked as if a marina had sprung up on the river.

The people who had rescued me had a long-distance hailer. It was more powerful than the one we had been using, which was now at the bottom of the river. "HEY!" My voice thundered across the water. "HEY! Friends of the Cougar! Count off!"

We had practised this routine just yesterday during a short-lived idea of being cheerleaders in an endangered species pep rally.

"COUNT OFF, I SAID!"

"One!" cried a voice from somewhere in the crowd of boats. "Two!" "Three!" "Four!"

There was a long pause. Then, "Five!" shouted the last quintuplet.

Every member of that maritime traffic jam roared, cheered, stamped, or whistled. Only then did I notice the mob on shore. Members of the household staff hung from every window of the official residence. People poured out across the lawn. Wilton clung to the branch of an apple tree at the edge of the garden, straining his eyes toward us. Mrs. Gummidge says he didn't cheer when the last quintuplet counted off. He just stood white-faced and furious, clenching and unclenching his fingers.

I cleared my throat again. The sound boomed through the long-distance hailer, and this made everyone look at me expectantly, as if they were waiting for me to say something. There seemed only one thing to do. Giving no sign that we had recently escaped a watery grave, I delivered the address on the plight of the eastern cougar. I will not repeat it here. You probably saw it in *Outdoors* or in *Survival Canada* or in one of the many newspapers that reprinted it the next day.

My speech seemed to touch the hearts of the rescuers and gawkers around me. Nobody seemed to mind—or even to notice—that the eastern cougar of which I spoke was actually a very subdued house cat, shrunk to a quarter of her actual size, with the dye from her blue collar staining her wet fur. It was unfortunate that one helpful woman had wrapped the shivering cat in a brand new, bright red sweatshirt. For many days afterward, Fluffy would be a pink cat with a startling blue ruff.

"WILTON AMARYLLIS!" I called when I finished the speech. "FLUFFY IS FINE. THANK YOU ALL FOR LISTENING."

Gummy says Wilton didn't express overwhelming relief at this announcement. Instead, he gave the tree branch such a shake that it shed a tumble of leaves. Then he threw down the hoe and stalked away without a word.

My mother, on the other hand, ran forward to join the people who were waiting to receive us on shore. I don't need to describe the mixture of scolding and hugging that greeted us.

As I told Mrs. Gummidge after dinner that night, "The people who rescued us from the water almost had to rescue us again!"

❦ ❦ ❦

We were in Gummy's sitting room. I was drinking my third cup of hot chocolate and licking marshmallow foam from my upper lip. Fluffy purred beside me on the sofa, apparently unaware of her bizarre coloring.

"She looks fluffier than ever now that she's dry," I said.

"As do *you*," replied Mrs. Gummidge. "What on *earth* came over you?"

"Gummy, haven't you heard of people who take incredible risks to help endangered animals?" I asked. "Haven't you heard of Greenpeace and their ship the *Rainbow Warrior?*"

She wrinkled her forehead at me.

"You know. They save whales and dolphins. Everyone knows about them," I said.

"So," she answered, "you needed your own ship. Is that it?"

"Well, yes. Something to get people's attention."

"You certainly did *that.*"

I laughed. "We certainly made a *splash.*"

She put one hand over her heart and closed her eyes. "It's not a joking matter. You frightened us nearly to death. Six of you in a boat made for *three,* and not a single life jacket."

"We were fine," I grumbled.

"Do you think you can tell a kidnapper just by looking?" she persisted. "Don't you know that anyone on those boats could have been one? And with the six of you so far from shore, we would have been powerless. Absolutely powerless."

"They didn't *kidnap* us," I protested. "They *rescued* us."

Wilton Amaryllis chose this inopportune moment to appear in the doorway.

"Mr. Sweetwine wants *her,*" he said, nodding stiffly in my direction. His face was red and furious. "Me and him have been having a little chat."

For a few seconds he seemed to fill the whole sitting room, towering over me. Then, like an angel flittering down from heaven, Nanny Grayson appeared behind him.

"Telephone, Willa," she said. "It's your father."

I drew my dignity around me, lifted my chin, and brushed

past Wilton. I even managed to say in a voice full of regal disdain, "I guess Mr. Sweetwine will just have to wait."

Wilton's face went as purple as the strip around Fluffy's dye-stained throat.

My father had seen the news reports.

After I had said, "No, I'm fine. Really," and "They made it look worse than it was," and "I'm okay," about fifty times, he heaved a huge sigh.

I could picture him pulling at his eyebrows and straightening his glasses. There was a clunk as he planted his elbows on the counter beside the cash register, and a clink-clink as he finished stirring his tea and tapped the spoon twice on the rim of his cup.

"Well," he said. "That's all right, then." Then he chuckled.

"What, Dad?"

"You're a chip off the old block, Willie. You dream big, don't you? Like your old dad?"

I grinned and said, "I guess so."

"You sure got their attention."

"Yeah."

"You'll go far. You've got the knack."

I wanted to ask exactly how far he thought I'd go, but he said, "How's your mother, Willie?"

"Fine," I replied. "I guess I scared her a little bit."

"Hmm. I guess so. Does she ask about me? Does she say anything about your old dad?"

"Sure. Sure, Dad."

It wasn't exactly a lie. Every morning when a member of the office staff brought the mail to the breakfast table, my mother placed her coffee cup in its saucer, raised her eyebrows toward the silver basket stuffed with envelopes, and asked casually, as if she'd just thought of it, "By the way, were there any postcards from my ex-husband?"

The staff member would say, "Yes, ma'am. A hundred and fourteen this morning," or whatever number it was. Sometimes a quintuplet, unable to help it, would giggle out loud.

My mother would silence this outburst with her beautiful frown, say, "Oh," in an airy way, pick up her cup again, and flip idly through the basket of letters, which came from people who wanted to ask for help, to offer advice, or just to tell my mother how lovely and inspiring she was.

The postcards, which were never included in the silver basket, accumulated at an incredible rate. The office staff kept them in a plastic crate in the library anteroom. My mother pretended not to care about them, but twice I'd surprised her in the anteroom, where she'd been gazing into the rapidly filling crate like someone trying to figure out a difficult crossword puzzle.

"The new system is going well, then?" asked my father.

"Oh." I said airily. "It's a success."

"I saw the write-up in the *National Tattletale,*" my father said drily. "And there was a piece in the *Gazette* this morning about my postcard campaign. I seem to be getting quite famous for my schemes."

He said this in such a dry funny voice that I grinned into the receiver.

"Mr. Sweetwine is furious. He says it's a scandal. He can't figure out who's telling the *Tattletale* about our private life."

"Hm," said my father. "Willie, you didn't phone the newspapers, did you?"

"Of course not!" I protested. "You don't think I would do something like that, do you?"

"If you did," he said, "I just hope you'd tell your old dad all about it."

"But . . ." I had to stop and choke back a rush of tears that sneaked up and surprised me. "I didn't. I *didn't.*"

"All right."

It was harder to stop those tears than I had expected. While I struggled to push them down, there was a silence. My throat ached.

"Willie?"

"People keep blaming me for things!" I burst out. "I didn't *do* anything!" Then I was weeping.

"Willie . . . stop . . . I'm not blaming you. Who's blaming you?"

"They hate me," I sobbed.

"What do you mean?"

"They hid Nanny's letter in my room and said I did it! And when Mr. Sweetwine read in the newspaper about the postcards, he started . . . he started . . . *looking* at me! But I didn't tell the newspapers. I didn't do *anything!*"

"I know you didn't. Of course you didn't, Willie," said my father, and I felt a little better.

"You'll come and see me soon," he said. "You ask them if you can come and see me for a little while."

"They won't let me."

"You ask them," said my father. "Don't cry."

"I'm not," I sobbed.

I loved the sound of his warm laugh. I tightened my grip on the receiver, wiped the tears from my face with the palm of my hand, and laughed shakily back at him.

"Oh," he said, "that's better, now."

I cleared my throat and sniffed. I wanted to ask him what he had meant about how I was going to go far and what kind of a knack I had and so on. But my father sighed and said, "Well, here comes Madame Tremblay for those azaleas. I must run. I'm glad you're all right, Willie. No more swimming in the river, now."

I let out a long breath and said, "Okay, Dad."

He said, "Ta, Willie," the way he always does, and hung up.

Chapter 17

The quints amazed me.

When the adults lined us up for the interrogation, the quints lowered their eyes, folded their hands in front of them, and refused to answer.

Mr. Sweetwine took the gentle approach. Flanked on one side by my mother and by a big sad-looking security agent on the other, he cleared his throat, studied his daughters, and said, "Now, I've played some youthful pranks in my time, and I appreciate what you tried to do out there on the river, but I want you to know that I am very worried about your safety. Leaving aside the lifejackets and overcrowded boat and so on, let's discuss how you managed to leave the grounds without permission."

My lips were sealed. But then, I was a veteran of this kind of thing. I didn't flinch, even though my heart was beating like a wild creature under my purple *Why Be Normal?* sweater. I folded my fingers tightly together, wondering how long it would take for the quints to blurt out the awful truth.

Nobody spoke.

"I would like to know," Mr. Sweetwine insisted, as if we had not understood him the first time, "how you made your way down to the river."

The quints looked down. Nobody moved. Marianne swiveled her eyes toward me, then inspected her fingernails.

"We're not angry, darlings," said my mother.

"No," echoed Mr. Sweetwine. "No, of course not. We're not angry."

Still, nobody spoke.

"Not in the slightest," said Mr. Sweetwine.

"We'd just like to know, for your own safety," said my mother in her most reasonable voice, "how you managed to get off the grounds." She smiled in a conspiratorial way. "It was very clever of you."

I held my breath. This was exactly the kind of thing that reduced the quintuplets to watery oatmeal, and my mother knew it. She left her chair and came to crouch in front of Marianne. She closed her slim fingers around Marianne's wrist.

"Darling," she said.

I swallowed against a sense of doom.

My mother beamed a smile like a blossoming rose into Marianne's uneasy face. "I can't for the life of me think how you managed it. Did you climb over the fence?"

"Not over *that* fence, they didn't," insisted the sad-faced security agent, causing my mother to stop and glance sharply at him.

Marianne took the opportunity to meet my eyes. I blinked. It seemed for an odd moment that she might be holding back a grin. This seemed so unlikely that I felt sure I'd imagined it.

"Marianne," my mother coaxed, "you know you can tell me everything, don't you?"

Marianne paid exquisite attention to the tops of her shoes.

"And there's nothing to be afraid of, no matter how many threats Willa might have made against you," my mother continued.

"Hey!" I yelped, "I didn't . . . why do you always accuse *me?*"

But the quints were staunch. They were stouthearted. They stood fast. They amazed me.

Mr. Sweetwine couldn't understand it. He humphed. He shifted uneasily in his chair. He leaned way over and whispered something to the security agent, who shrugged. And all the time, my mother coaxed, cajoled, and implored. The more the quints resisted, the huffier Mr. Sweetwine became until he could no longer sit still. He slapped his hands flat on the desk, rose from his seat, and bellowed, "That's enough!"

It was the worst thing he could have done. The quints jumped. They gawked at him with big startled eyes.

"Now I want to know how you did it, and I want to know *now!*"

It was terrifying. Even *I* had to clench my fists against his shouting. Beside me, Marianne had gone rigid with nerves.

"Suzanne!" he yelled. "You tell me!"

It must have taken everything she had, but she did it. She looked hard at the edge of his desk, tensed her jaw, and waited fiercely. She did not utter a single word.

"I don't believe it!" He was as furious as he'd been when that important tax bill was defeated in Parliament. Maybe worse. My mother made little calming motions toward him, like someone guiding a plane in for an emergency landing.

But Mr. Sweetwine shook his head. He'd moved beyond yelling, into soft-voiced disappointment. He swung his head toward Marianne, fixed her with a searing gaze, and said quietly, "Marianne, I'm going to count to three. One . . ."

Her bottom lip wobbled. I closed my eyes.

"Two."

She hiccuped.

"Three," he said.

She burst into tears. I could tell from her first enormous shuddering breath that she had no intention of skimping on the hysterics. She buried her face in her hands. She sobbed so hard her bones seemed to joggle in their sockets. Her thin shoulder blades stuck out like the wings of a baby bird, convulsing with each heaving breath.

Mr. Sweetwine stared. The security agent coughed and straightened his collar.

"Oh dear," said my mother. She opened her arms to Marianne.

There was another hiccuping sob. And another. It wasn't long before my mother's arms were full of weeping quintuplets. There were so many tears pouring out of them that my mother's face and throat were soon as wet and blotchy as theirs. Every time the crying slowed down, a quint would gulp out another heart-wrenching sob, and they would all start up again.

"This is ridiculous!" Mr. Sweetwine hollered over the noise. "Can't you make them stop?"

Eventually, my mother did, with many kind pats and murmurs of encouragement, handfuls of Kleenex, and hopeful smiles. "All right," she said at last. "We'll say no more about it. But I want you to promise me one thing."

The quints drew shivering breaths and watched her warily with wet brown eyes.

"Promise me you'll never do it again."

They were so relieved they practically howled out their promises. They fell into her arms with happy tears and joyful apologies. I stood stiffly, apart from them, feeling cold.

My mother looked at me across that armful of smooth, dark heads, and I wanted to run. I curled my hands into tight fists and swallowed hard against the rage that was rising inside me.

"I promise," I echoed in a flat voice.

She *almost* smiled at me with her eyes. Then she nodded briskly and turned to exchange a glance with Mr. Sweetwine. He shrugged, rolled his eyes toward the ceiling, and slumped into his big leather chair, shaking his head.

Later that evening, when the quints were busy playing Scrabble with my mother, I sneaked into their moonlit room, searched until I found the *Happy Dooley* book under somebody's bathrobe, and stole it back.

I hid it in the back of my closet, in the cardboard box with my winter boots, under my empty suitcase.

Chapter 18

It wasn't my fault. In fact, I didn't even know I was eavesdropping until Mrs. Gummidge said the word *poop,* which naturally made my ears swivel around.

At the time, I was engaged in a most interesting venture, which involved kneeling in front of the TV in my mother's bedroom for long periods and feeding tapes into the VCR. When I heard my mother coming up the front stairs, there was no time to get away. I just hunkered down a bit lower behind the ottoman to make myself less noticeable and hoped she would pass by without coming into her bedroom. But when I heard her stop and say, "Mrs. Gummidge?" and "How are things going in the kitchen?" and "I've been meaning to ask you about something," and when I heard Mrs. Gummidge using the word *poop,* naturally I started to listen.

What Gummy had actually said was, "Don't worry about Wilton Amaryllis, ma'am. He can be a bit of an old poop."

My mother laughed in that lilting voice and said, "I don't suppose it's easy for him, taking orders from me. He's been making his own decisions about the landscaping for a very long time."

"That's right," said Mrs. Gummidge.

"I hope he doesn't think I'd ever jeopardize his position here. I hope he doesn't feel redundant."

"I wouldn't know," said Mrs. Gummidge.

"I just wondered," my mother persisted, "whether he might be afraid of losing his job. I had heard . . . something . . . about his financial situation."

Gummy didn't answer. She shifted her weight awkwardly. I heard her knees creak.

"Mrs. Gummidge?" I knew my mother must be tipping her head to one side, listening in that way that made it almost impossible for the other person to stay silent.

"He's under a bit of pressure lately," Mrs. Gummidge admitted grudgingly. "Trying to scrape together a down payment. So they say."

My mother didn't ask who "they" were. She said, "Is he trying to buy a house, then?"

"Yes, ma'am," said Mrs. Gummidge. "The family home. His brother wants to sell it. Turn it into condominiums."

"Oh dear," said my mother.

"Wilton was born there," said Mrs. Gummidge. "Grew up in that house. So I hear. He may come across as a grumpy old man, but he's got a soft spot for that house. It would just about kill him to see it broken up and sold off. So I hear."

"So *that's* it," said my mother.

"That's just what I hear," said Gummy. "I can't say more about it."

"Of course not," said my mother.

"So he'll be counting on a steady salary," Gummy went on, in a rush, as if she were afraid she'd said too much. "That's all. Well. I'd better get on back to . . ."

"Yes," said my mother vaguely. "I've already tried to put his mind at ease about that. I wish I knew what else I could do."

Mrs. Gummidge started toward the stairs, but my mother stopped her. Inwardly, I groaned. I was getting a cramp in my left foot and longed to stand up and stretch it out. I wished I could fling myself into the corridor, shouting, "That's enough, you two. Quit gossiping. And get away from each other."

I didn't, of course. I was running down a mental checklist of the things my mother might say if she caught me hiding behind the ottoman in her bedroom with five video cassettes, a pad of typing paper filched from Mr. Sweetwine's office, and two half-eaten chocolate chip cookies. I wasn't eager to find out.

"Oh dear," said my mother, laughing girlishly. Mrs. Gummidge did not laugh back. "I hope you won't think I'm sticking my nose into other people's affairs."

She waited for Mrs. Gummidge to say that of course she wasn't. Gummy didn't say anything.

"It's just," said my mother, "that I wonder if there might be something bothering Nan . . . Pauline Grayson?"

Mrs. Gummidge made a humming noise. "In what way, ma'am?"

"Well, I've just found her in the pantry in tears," said my mother. "She won't tell me what's wrong."

"Oh dear," said Gummy.

"Maybe you'd like to go down and have a word."

"Yes," said Gummy. "Perhaps I will. Thank you."

They made let's-wrap-it-up noises and shuffled their feet. The cramp in my leg was getting worse. Gummy hurried off down the stairs, and I held my breath, willing my mother to pass right by her bedroom.

It worked. As soon as she wandered away down the corridor, I danced an impromptu polka around her room to get the pins and needles out of my foot.

Marianne didn't seem to think anything of it. If I hadn't specifically gossiped about Nanny Grayson, I don't think Marianne even would have bothered to tell me what happened.

We were busy at the table in the playroom, with a box of postcards and stickers, holding pencils that had formed the same words so many times that they seemed to scribble along by themselves. Through the big playroom windows, we could see the flat silver river sweeping past the foot of the garden. The late afternoon sun shone into it like a brass coin. For once I wasn't surrounded by stepsisters. While Marianne and I worked, the others were busy swimming laps in the indoor pool. The playroom seemed like a cool glass bubble in the middle of the hot afternoon.

"Did you know Nanny Grayson was crying? After lunch today?" I asked, licking a sticker and applying it neatly to a postcard. Later, I would carry a satisfyingly thick packet of these down to the library and slip them in with the rest of the day's mail. I loved the weight of them, and the delicious clunk they made when they hit the silver tray.

"What?" said Marianne.

"I heard someone say Nanny Grayson was crying in the pantry," I said. I expected Marianne to ask why and me to say I didn't know and then both of us to imagine a few dozen reasons why the unflappable Nanny Grayson might end up blubbering among the groceries. I expected us to have a chummy little conversation about it.

Instead, Marianne looked up and said, "Yes, she was."

"What?"

"I was there," said Marianne. "I saw her."

She stopped to erase a mistake, and for a ridiculous moment she seemed to think that was the end of the conversation.

Someone had to ask the obvious question, so I said, "Why was she?"

"I don't know," said Marianne placidly. "Mrs. Gummidge made me go find Nick Andrews and tell him Nanny was crying."

I glared at her. I thought she was joking. But she went on carefully pushing her pencil up and down, forming neat round quintuplet letters.

"Then what?" I persisted in an exasperated voice.

"What do you mean?"

"I mean, did he come? Did he ask her why she was crying?" I was practically yelling. I glanced at the open door and lowered my voice. "Did you notice anything . . . suspicious . . . about the two of them?"

"Who?"

I rolled my eyes upward, threw my pencil on the table, and pushed back my chair.

"He couldn't come," said Marianne.

"He couldn't?"

"No. He said to tell her he would meet her after dinner."

"After dinner tonight?"

"Yes." She scratched the tip of her nose, looked out over the river, and selected another postcard from the box. "He said to tell her he would meet her after dinner. At the lobster pot."

Chapter 19

I recruited Marianne. I'd discovered that beneath her mousy exterior she had some remarkable talents. For example, Marianne could stand beside you like a soldier while you were being yelled at. The tears might tremble on her eyelashes, and her breath might come in tight gasps, but she could hold back even the worst fit of crying until she was perfectly alone with a pillow and a handful of Kleenex. On the other hand, when a few tears were called for, nobody else could turn on the weeping so suddenly and in such a heart-wrenching manner. When Marianne let go with the hysterics, everyone in the room had to yank out a Kleenex. She was very versatile.

It was Marianne who looked up *lobster pot* in the illustrated dictionary and showed me the picture. This was extremely helpful, as I had planned to look for lobster pots in the kitchen cupboard. Instead, at seven o'clock, she and I crouched down behind the cedar hedge near the Maritime garden with a tape recorder and a police whistle that we planned to use in case we needed to summon help. Through the fragrant cedar branches I could see the bottom edge of the lobster trap (or lobster *pot*, as they're sometimes called), which my mother had placed on a rock. I could see the fishing net she'd draped artistically over a hunk of driftwood and the lobster buoy she'd dangled nearby.

It was a perfectly secluded spot for a secret rendezvous.

"Here he comes," whispered Marianne.

It was Nick. He settled himself on a big barnacle-covered rock. He did not look like a criminal. He looked like someone in an after-shave commercial. He leaned forward with his elbows on his knees, gazed happily out over the river, and hummed a few bars of "Row, Row, Row Your Boat."

Nanny Grayson was a few minutes late. She hurried up the gravel path with quick crunching footsteps, put her arms around Nick's neck, and kissed him.

My mouth dropped open. Marianne clasped both hands over her face to keep from laughing out loud. It wasn't until I scowled and gestured that she remembered to turn on the tape recorder.

She did it just in time. The evidence came faster and more clearly than either of us expected. Still, it was a shock. I had *suspected* that the two of them were up to no good, but to hear them actually planning a crime was terrifying. And to be there, listening and recording it, was even more thrilling than you might imagine.

Nick said, "I didn't think they'd catch on so soon. I miscalculated." He kissed Nanny Grayson again. From our leafy bower all we could see were her gray pumps and Nick's running shoes, but when she went up on her toes we knew he was smooching her, and we resisted an almost overwhelming fit of the giggles.

"Mr. and Mrs. Sweetwine don't suspect anything," Nanny replied. "I know that for a fact."

There was a gloomy pause. Then Nick said, "I thought my job with security would make it easier for us to get away with it. But now I suspect that the rest of the security staff is onto us. Someone's trying to trick us into revealing our plans."

"Who?"

"I don't know," he said in a flat discouraged voice. "But I got another message on my answering machine, threatening to turn me in to the sergeant. It's blackmail. We're being blackmailed."

Like Marianne, I pushed my knuckles into my mouth.

"I was sure Willa was up to something," said Nanny. "But maybe you're right. Maybe it's someone on the security staff." Her voice rose to a panicky note and hung there. "Wilton said one of the guards saw Willa take that letter from my room, but . . . what if someone you work with has found out about us? What if they report us?"

"We'll just have to move our plans forward," said Nick with a soft smacking sound we knew to be another kiss. "There's nothing anyone can do to stop us. Once we're out of town—out of the line of fire—we can forget all this and get on with our lives."

"You want to do it soon? When?"

"I was thinking the end of the week. Say next Friday at 6:00 P.M. I don't think we can afford to wait any longer."

"Oh, Nick," she said in a small nervous voice. "Are you sure we can't . . ."

"Don't panic, now," he replied. "This is no time to lose our heads. I'll go on ahead. Once I'm in Toronto I can set up a nice private hide-out. We'll get some toys and some kid-sized furniture. Everything will be all right."

"Toys and *furniture?* Do you really think it's going to be that simple?"

"Well, I guess I'm going to find out in the near future, aren't I?" he joked in a voice that made my blood run cold. "All we need are the basics. I'll manage."

"I'll come with you," she said.

"No. You work until the last minute. We'll need the money. We can't afford to go changing our plans this far into the game."

There was a brief pause. Nanny sniffed.

"Pauline," said Nick. "Don't cry. As soon as I'm out of the way, things will calm down." There was a silence.

"I'm worried about this business with the tabloids," said Nanny. "It's practically impossible to cover up anything around here. We'll have to be very careful."

"We will. I'll book the train ticket under a false name. Then we'll lay low for a while. It'll give us a chance to get everything ready before D-Day." Nick laughed in a low voice. I opened my eyes wide and found Marianne looking at me with a horrified expression.

"Here," Nick went on, rustling a sheet of paper. "I've written it already. You want to check it over?"

Silence. My heart tripped and raced. I closed one fist tight around my collar and mouthed the words "ransom note" at Marianne.

She mouthed back, "What?"

"Do you really think," said Nanny, "you should say that you demand the money? Shouldn't you say you *request* that it be sent to you at the earliest convenience?"

Marianne's eyes bulged. She mouthed "ransom note?" and

I bobbed my head up and down, clutching my collar even tighter.

Nick laughed. "You really think politeness counts in this situation?" Silence. Then we heard Nick saying, "Oh no. I was just teasing. Don't cry."

I exchanged a meaningful glance with Marianne, who was leaning over the tape recorder like a sound engineer, making sure it was still recording this appalling evidence.

"Don't worry so much," said Nick. "We can pull this off without a hitch."

More smooching. After a while—roughly the length of time it would take to eat one of Gummy's five-course meals—Nanny sighed and said in a regretful voice, "Look, I have to get going. They'll be expecting me in the playroom, and it would ruin everything if they blew the whistle on us now."

I fingered the police whistle and considered it, but Marianne shook her head at me.

"I was thinking," said Nanny, "that I could come meet you in Toronto in a couple of weeks. I could tell Mr. Sweetwine there was a family emergency."

"Family emergency," Nick snorted. "There's going to be a family emergency all right."

There was a strange moment of silence, during which Marianne and I craned our heads so far into the cedar hedge that the boughs scraped our faces.

"Nick," said Nanny. "You're not . . . you're not having second thoughts about this whole thing, are you?"

"You're kidding, right?"

"It's just . . . you know, there's no going back. It's all or nothing after this. And I don't want to feel that I dragged you into it."

"Listen," he said teasingly, "you've just got cold feet. Once the whole thing is over and we're safe in Toronto, everything will be fine."

She must have given him a funny look because he laughed and said, "We're partners now. Right?"

She said, "All right," and went up on her toes for several boring minutes that lasted so long Marianne actually had to put the tape on pause.

Then Nanny said quietly, "Friday at six, then. You'll take care of your part of the plan, right?"

Nick laughed again. "I know the plan like the back of my hand. It's just the timing that's different. Have we talked about anything else over the last four weeks?" There was a little pause. "We probably shouldn't be seen together too much before then. Okay?"

More kissing. Then Nanny fled down the path, sending up little spurts of gravel from her heels. Nick slouched away toward the gate, humming "Row, Row, Row Your Boat" while gazing dreamily across the river.

As soon as he disappeared around the side of the official residence, Marianne snatched up the tape recorder. We flew back to the house and flung ourselves into my room.

"Did it work? Did we get it?" I gasped.

We listened to the tape from beginning to end. Some of the conversation was drowned out by the shudder of the river breeze across the microphone. But most of the words were clear.

"We can't be making a mistake on this, can we?" I demanded. "I mean, they really are talking about blackmail? Maybe even kidnapping?"

Marianne, with her eyes wide and her lungs short of breath from all the running, said, "I don't see how we could be wrong. They're definitely up to no good. And we've got times, dates, everything."

"You'll come with me to tell your dad," I persisted.

"Yes," she said.

We didn't waste another moment. We clattered down the stairs and across the tiled hall, threw open the doors to the living room where my mother and Mr. Sweetwine were sipping after-dinner drinks with the Governor General and a few other neighbors, and barged into the middle of one of Mr. Sweetwine's long-winded anecdotes.

Conversation stopped.

I drew a deep breath and told all.

🍁 🍁 🍁

When we blurted out that we had discovered criminals beside the lobster pot in the Maritime garden, even Mr. Sweetwine panicked. My mother clapped a hand to her necklace as if to prevent it from flying off, and the assembled dignitaries froze

112

like people in a flash photo. Someone raced off to alert the security staff. The maid, trembling, slipped past us and hurried toward the kitchen to deliver the awful news to Mrs. Gummidge.

Marianne and I were already dragging Mr. Sweetwine toward the library. My mother stood up to follow, but her husband looked at her over our heads and said, "Will you please find the quints and stay with them?" My mother's blue eyes flicked across me like a feather duster. Then she closed her hand more tightly around her necklace and hurried up to the playroom.

Within seconds, red-coated Mounties were pouring through the lower entryway. Their shiny boots creaked on the tiles. Their tall hats seemed to brush door frames and chandeliers, and their footsteps shuddered on the staircase. Two Mounties stood like statues inside the library door until a couple of worried security agents burst in with their jackets flapping.

"Close the door," said Mr. Sweetwine.

We played him the tape recording. As he finished listening, the prime minister's face sagged like the face of an exhausted beagle. He sank deep into his big leather chair.

"If I hadn't heard it with my own ears," he said, "I wouldn't have believed it. All right. I want you to go find these two and bring them . . ."

"Sir."

The Mountie behind me strode forward from his position near the door. He cleared his throat and said, "I have some information which may help, sir." The rims of his ears were as red as his jacket.

But before Mr. Sweetwine could reply, there was a scuffle and a bang outside the door. Someone yanked the handle, and Mrs. Gummidge burst into our midst. She was as ruffled and furious as an angry hen. Behind her stood Nanny Grayson, whose stricken face seemed to be carved out of stone.

Mrs. Gummidge hustled forward and loomed over me in her fuzzy lavender cardigan. When she shook her strong finger at me, I cowered. The Mountie flashed out his arm to prevent her from hitting me, but of course she had no intention of doing that. She turned a piercing look on him and he stepped back, blushing more furiously than ever.

"Willa, aren't you *ashamed* of yourself?" she demanded. "Is it true that you are behind this . . . this *outrage?*"

I did not know how to answer the question. Marianne sat up straight and hung on tightly to the arms of her chair. The uneasy feeling started to come over both of us at the same time, and I dared to sneak a look at Mr. Sweetwine. So did Mrs. Gummidge. She smoothed a gray curl back from her flushed cheek.

"Sir," she said, "it has come to my attention that a terrible accusation has been made against Ms. Grayson and . . . and . . . a certain young man."

"Nick Andrews," said Mr. Sweetwine, narrowing his eyes as if in his powerful mind the embarrassing truth was beginning to unfurl itself.

"Well, sir, I don't know what these two . . . *children* . . . overheard, but I can assure you there's been a terrible mistake."

Marianne lifted her eyelids so I could see right into her round unhappy eyes.

"We have a tape," I offered uneasily.

"Good lord!" Mrs. Gummidge clasped her hands across the front of her cardigan and closed her eyes. She sucked a deep breath, whooshed it out, and flapped an impatient hand at Nanny Grayson.

"All right, Pauline," she said. "Come right here and tell them everything." She pointed at the Mountie. "You. Close the door."

He did.

Nanny Grayson faced Mr. Sweetwine like someone who has been called to the principal's office and said, "As Arabella . . . I mean, as Mrs. Gummidge . . . has said, there's been a terrible misunderstanding. When we heard that the children had overheard k-kidnappers and b-blackmailers . . ." She looked at me with a hot gaze. Tears shone on her lashes, and my heart squeezed tight. "Well," she went on, "I knew they'd heard my conversation with Nick and . . . jumped to the wrong conclusion."

Mr. Sweetwine rubbed his ear. He turned his gold pen over and over on the desk blotter. He tapped it on the tape recorder.

"I have," he said uncomfortably, "heard the conversation."

Nanny Grayson made a noise and covered her face with both hands.

"And while I would certainly never condone this type of eavesdropping," said Mr. Sweetwine, "the conversation could . . . what I mean to say is . . . not that we can excuse this snooping or

114

whatever you might call it, but the false names, the train tickets, the lying, and . . . well, so on."

He puffed. He was exhausted.

Nanny Grayson couldn't speak. Mrs. Gummidge clucked and patted her on the shoulder.

"Sir," interrupted the Mountie. He was alert, staring out the window at something or someone who seemed to be advancing up the driveway at great speed.

Footsteps pounded in the lower entryway, slapped across the hall, and squeaked to a halt on the tiles. The library door flew open and struck the bookshelves with a bang that made even the Mounties jump.

Nick didn't hesitate. He rushed in, rumpled and red-faced from running, and shouldered his way through the crowd until he was standing right in front of the prime minister's desk. When Nanny Grayson saw him, she cried out again and put her hands over her mouth.

"This is ridiculous!" Nick yelled at Mr. Sweetwine. "Who dreamed this up? We don't know anything about a kidnapping!"

I sank lower in my chair.

"Then, Mr. Andrews," said Mr. Sweetwine. "What . . . ?"

"We're getting *married!*" Nick hollered. "All right? We're running away to get *married!* There's your big terrible crime!"

I thought Marianne's eyes would fall out of her head and go rolling around on the floor. My own eyes felt strange. Everything seemed unbearably bright.

Nanny Grayson wiped her face with her hands.

"It's true," she said in a shaky voice. "We've been planning it for a while. We didn't mean to deceive anyone, but there has been so much scandal in the last little while, and we didn't want to make things worse by giving the tabloids anything to print."

"In fact, someone on staff has been spying on us," Nick added, taking her in his arms as she began to sob.

"Trying to force Nick to quit his job," she said through her tears. "Blackmailing us."

"Good God," said Mr. Sweetwine.

"Yes," Nick insisted, growing calmer. "I'm afraid I didn't handle it well. I don't know how things got so . . . out of hand."

"But," said Mr. Sweetwine, "there was a ransom note."

Nick made a sound that was more like a sob than a laugh and tugged a folded paper from the pocket of his jeans.

"My letter of resignation," he said flatly.

Mr. Sweetwine unfolded it carefully, read it from top to bottom, folded it up again, and handed it to Nick with a wry grin.

"The part where you *demand* your final pay might be worded a bit strongly," said Mr. Sweetwine. He tapped his pen on the desk blotter and said, "I wish you had come to me sooner. This uproar might have been avoided."

Nanny Grayson pressed her face into Nick's shoulder and howled.

"We were trying to avoid a scandal," Nick confessed, looking straight at Mr. Sweetwine as though he wanted to say more with his face than with his words. "We weren't sure you would approve of our . . . situation, and we knew someone on staff was leaking information to the media. We didn't want to risk any publicity that would reflect badly on you and your family."

Mr. Sweetwine still looked baffled, but Mrs. Gummidge was shuffling me out of the chair and urging Nanny Grayson into it with soothing clucks and pats that didn't do a thing to stop Nanny's weeping.

"We thought we could just slip away quietly. I was going to hand in my resignation next Friday," Nick said earnestly, "and go to Toronto to look for a job and an apartment. That way, everything would be settled before it became obvious that Pauline is . . ." He broke off and looked hard at his knuckles. Mr. Sweetwine's eyes had widened, and he stiffened.

"What's he talking about?" Marianne whispered.

"I think," I murmured back, "he means Nanny Grayson is going to have a baby."

I must have said it more loudly than I intended because Mrs. Gummidge flashed one of her annoyed looks at me. Mr. Sweetwine threw his pen onto the desk and rolled his eyes toward the ceiling. Nanny Grayson sobbed harder than ever.

But Marianne's confusion had given way to the most amazing transformation. Her lips shaped themselves around an inaudible, "Ohhhh . . ." Her eyes curved up into a delighted dazzle. It was as if her body became one huge smile. Before anyone else could step in, Marianne flung herself forward, wrapped her

116

thin arms around as much of Nanny Grayson as she could grab, and hugged with all her might.

"Is it true?" Marianne demanded, pulling back just enough to see Nanny's hysterical nod before she encircled her again with her fierce little arms.

"Then why are you crying?" Marianne persisted. "I'm sorry for what we did. We're both sorry, aren't we, Willa? But you don't have to cry anymore, Nanny. It's all right now."

Nanny Grayson hugged her back.

"It's all right now, isn't it, Daddy?" Marianne insisted. "Isn't it?"

"Hummm," said Mr. Sweetwine.

His daughter scrutinized him with bewildered eyes. The look softened him immediately.

"Of course it's all right," he said. "All the same, I think it would be a good idea for Mr. Andrews and Ms. Grayson to carry out their plans. Perhaps take an extended . . ."

"Nothing could stop us," Nick said, lifting his chin proudly, "from carrying out our plans."

"Then let's discuss them," Mr. Sweetwine suggested, "in a less public interview."

Practically everybody realized he wanted us to leave. Even Marianne untangled herself from her ecstatic embrace and fixed Nanny Grayson with another thrilled gaze.

"Will you let me hold the baby?" she begged. "After it's born, can I be the first one to hold it?"

Nanny Grayson laughed through her tears and gave Marianne a gentle shake. "You can hold it as often as you like, you remarkable child," she promised. Then she kissed the top of Marianne's head.

I needed to say something. I couldn't think what it was. And the timing seemed all wrong. Nick and Nanny were both showering Marianne with fond glances. I had the distinct feeling that no matter what I said, no matter how heartfelt it might be, nobody was going to kiss the top of *my* head.

So when Marianne had peeled herself away I just looked at them all—Mrs. Gummidge, Mr. Sweetwine, Nick, and Nanny. Then I gathered myself together and ran.

Chapter 20

Mr. Sweetwine was not pleased that Nick and Nanny had been sneaking around the official residence at night. He was not pleased that Nanny's attention was on Nick and Nick's attention was on Nanny at certain times when they were both supposed to be paying attention to the quintuplets and me. He didn't like it that Nanny was planning to leave us on such short notice and without a replacement Nanny to step into her shoes. And he didn't like the way she was planning to lie to him so she could sneak off to meet Nick in Toronto.

Mr. Sweetwine thought it would be best if Nick and Nanny went away immediately. It would give them more time, he said, to prepare for the wedding and the blessed event.

Gummy says it's important, before an election, to be magnanimous, which is why Mr. Sweetwine wished them well and even asked Mrs. Gummidge to prepare a small celebration for the family and staff, to say goodbye to Nick and Nanny.

It is not in Mrs. Gummidge's nature to prepare a *small* celebration. For two days, she did not sit in her sitting room. She did not spend any quiet moments in the pantry admiring her well-stocked shelves. She did not invite me to watch the evening news with her. Every time I tried to talk to her, she shooed me away or put me to work fetching or stirring or slicing.

On the day before the party, Marianne found me in the cook's sitting room, trying to load film into Gummy's old-fashioned camera. Unfortunately, I had bragged to Mrs. G. about how easy this would be. I had even implied, with certain gestures and facial expressions, that anyone who could not do it must be dim. By the time Marianne's anxious face appeared in the doorway, I'd been struggling with the camera for nearly half an hour.

"It's amazing," I said, "how many meters of film they can fit in this little container."

"Gummy's camera," Marianne observed, stepping carefully around the ribbons of film that twisted on the floor around my feet. "She only gets it out for special occasions."

"Yes. Well," I said, fiddling with a twiddly knob, "did you want me for something?"

"Um," she said.

I looked up.

"It's about that book," she said.

"What book?"

"The Happy Dooleys on . . ."

"Oh," I said, looking down again. "That one."

"I can't find it."

"Well. It doesn't matter."

"I've looked everywhere. I don't know what happened to it. I'm really sorry."

"Oh," I said. "Never mind. It was an awful book, anyway."

"Do you want me to ask your mother if she can help? Or buy you a new one?"

"No!" I nearly dropped the camera. "I mean, don't. Please. Just forget about it. It doesn't matter."

"Okay," she said in a doubting voice and dropped the subject.

🍁 🍁 🍁

When the party was over, when everyone had gobbled the pastries and pies and cookies, when we had swallowed down the bowls and pitchers of punch and tucked away slabs of cake with ice cream, Mrs. Gummidge accepted our praise with a casual little smile and a polite nod.

The next thing I knew, the quints were showering Nick and Nanny with hysterical tears and enfolding them in quintuplet-ish embraces. Mr. Sweetwine slapped Nick on the shoulder and pumped his arm up and down and made the quintuplets squeal by kissing Nanny Grayson on the cheek. Meanwhile, Mrs. Gummidge fluttered around the edges of the crowd like a large turquoise moth. Her nose was red, and when she thought we weren't looking she dabbed at her eyes with a Kleenex she had hidden up the cuff of her sweater.

My mother said she planned to take her time and hire an ideal new nanny for us. In the meantime, my mother and Mrs. Gummidge would look after us. But a new Mountie had already been recruited to fill Nick's job at the gatehouse, and as we gazed down the driveway at him, Mrs. Gummidge confided to me between sniffs, "I hear he's a hotshot. Wilton Amaryllis says he's the golden-haired boy of the police academy."

When Nick and Nanny hurried down the steps to the car, everyone followed them, talking all at once. Everyone, that is, except Mrs. Gummidge, who had stepped back into a corner of the lower entryway and was pressing the Kleenex to her upper lip.

I pushed past the boy-faced Mountie, ran down the remaining couple of steps to the waiting car, and closed my fingers around the shiny silver handle. The clamor of voices poured down the steps, running into the yard.

When Nanny got close enough, I clutched at her hand. She looked down at me, startled, which made Nick stop talking to Mr. Sweetwine and look down at me, too.

"I just wanted to say . . ." I said.

Nanny's face changed. She studied me the way she sometimes puzzles over a poem or a math problem. Thoughtfully. Carefully. She waited.

"I'm sorry," I said. "I'm sorry I spied on you."

That was all. I stopped, watching to see whether she would yell at me or burst out laughing or make a sarcastic remark or push herself away from me.

But she just put her hand on my shoulder, shook me gently, and said, "Don't worry about it." Nick grinned and turned away to continue his conversation with Mr. Sweetwine.

It was as if a storm of white birds had broken loose in my heart. I grabbed Nanny, kissed her hard on the cheek, and said, "And I'm sorry I thought you and Nick were blackmailers."

"If we're apologizing about that," she said, "then I'm sorry I suspected you, too."

The quints were pushing around her, pulling her attention away from me with their adorable tear-stained faces and their chattering voices.

"Don't worry," I told her hastily as the deluge of quints swamped me. "I'm going to find out who blackmailed you."

Nanny laughed. "If anyone can do it, you can," she said.

I wanted to run madly around the lawn, howling.

Instead, I raced up the stairs to the alcove where Mrs. Gummidge was standing, sniffing discreetly. I threw my arms around her and hugged her until she said, "Oof. Stop that." I stood beside her as the car pulled away down the driveway.

Nanny and Nick waved from the back seat, and we all waved back. Even the Mountie behind the wheel waved and grinned.

The new gatehouse guard saluted and opened the gate solemnly, the car turned onto Sussex Drive, and they were gone.

Chapter 21

Mrs. Gummidge didn't know I had contacted the CBC. Nobody did. As soon as the visitors crossed the hallway, and I realized what had happened, I raced to the door of Gummy's sitting room and gasped out, "You'll never guess who's here!"

Gummy merely raised an eyebrow.

"Gloria Fandango from the CBC News," I announced. "She just went into the living room!"

Mrs. Gummidge humphed. She says that after twenty-seven years at the official residence it takes more than the host of a national television show to impress her.

"She asked for a TV and VCR, and Mr. Sweetwine sent Wilton upstairs to get them," I said. "You'll never guess what's going on. . . . Are you coming?"

Mrs. Gummidge modified the raised eyebrow.

"I suppose they'll want coffee and cookies," she sniffed, and went to prepare them. I ran back upstairs to the playroom, where I thought the quints were busy drawing pictures of endangered animals, but my mother was alone there, sitting at the little table near the playroom window.

"They're in their bedroom," she said, "having that set of matching dresses fitted." She looked tired. The table and chair were too low for her, and when she leaned over to study Marianne's picture of the eastern cougar she seemed to droop more than usual. "What's happening downstairs? I saw Mr. Amaryllis carrying the TV set."

"Um," I said.

She looked at me with her bright blue eyes and began to

collect the drawings. The Children's Art Foundation was going to paste them in a scrapbook and auction it off to the highest bidder.

"You'd better come," I said.

She drew a deep breath, held it for a moment while she pressed her lips tightly together, and let it out in a sigh. "I'll be right there," she said. She used a voice that implied she had been pushed past the limits of human endurance.

Mrs. Gummidge, crossing the black and white tiles with a silver coffee tray, had changed her apron. We met in the hallway. Actually, we met in midair. I had launched myself from the fifth stair, which was my best jump so far. I landed with a flat-footed slap on the tiles. Mrs. Gummidge nearly dropped the tray.

"Good heavens."

"I'm working up to a whole flight of stairs," I explained. "So I jump one extra step every day. In two more weeks I'll be able to jump from the top."

"Good heavens," she said again. "You'll break your neck."

I accompanied her to the living room door with the nonchalance of someone who is used to rubbing elbows with national celebrities, but when I saw Gloria Fandango, my heart swooped and dived in my chest. I croaked, "Whoa. Hang on to your hat, Gummy."

The living room buzzed with conversation. Mr. Sweetwine was there, chatting with a man in a business suit. Sid, the new security guard, stood like a statue just inside the living room door, looking splendid in his Mountie uniform. Wilton Amaryllis, as gruff as always, busied himself with television cables and electrical outlets. One of the office staff hovered, smiling and exchanging pleasantries with Gloria Fandango herself.

"Hello." I struggled to sound cheerful and unconcerned, but my voice wavered. "What's going on? Are we going to *film* something?"

Mr. Sweetwine fixed his goodwill smile firmly in place. "No, my dear. We're going to *watch* something. Ms. Fandango called me today after Question Period to say you'd sent her a *surprise*. Ha-ha. And . . . ah, good . . . here's your mother."

The glory of the prime ministerial smile blazed around the room. In comparison, my mother's smile was little more than a flicker.

"Ms. Fandango," continued Mr. Sweetwine, "I'd like you to meet my stepdaughter. Willa, it seems you're familiar with Ms. Fandango's work."

I nodded. For once, I was speechless. My hand was in Gloria Fandango's slim, cool, manicured clasp. I looked into that oh-so-familiar face and felt I'd met a kindred spirit at last. Mrs. Gummidge said later that she found it refreshing to see that kind of hero worship in the official residence.

"Well, hello there," said Gloria Fandango. Her laughter was like water over pebbles. "It's a real pleasure to meet you, Willa. Your package caused quite a stir in my office."

My mind whirled. The silence lengthened. Mr. Sweetwine cast a desperate glance around the room.

"Coffee!" he observed brightly. "Splendid! Thank you, Mrs. Gummidge."

As Gummy began to serve, Ms. Fandango popped a video cassette into the machine.

"Before we go any farther, I'd like you to see the surprise your daughter sent me. Is this ready to go?"

Wilton Amaryllis finished tinkering with cables, nodded, glowered at me, and clumped away.

"Super," said Ms. Fandango. She pressed a button.

The nightly newscast gave way to a buzz, a few seconds of blank screen, and a rush of inspiring music. It was Handel's *Water Music,* actually. A shot of the river taken through the fence at the foot of the lawn dissolved into a close-up of my face.

"Oh, my God," said my mother.

The *me* on the screen grinned hugely.

"Behold the peaceful waters of the Ottawa River," said the voice that did not sound like mine. "Who could guess that *this* could so quickly become . . . *this.* "

My on-screen arm gestured toward the river. The picture changed. For a moment, there was only noise and confusion. Then, in a flash, the picture became clear—the Sweetwine children were being rescued from their watery doom. It was excellent footage, if I do say so myself. You may have noticed, as I did, that the news reports on the night of the near-drowning were full of video clips sent in by amateur photographers. Fortunately, I'd been able to sneak into my mother's bedroom and tape these, and they gave a dramatic look to my commercial message.

"Don't let this happen to you," my on-screen self advised. "We learned our lesson, so the Sweetwine quintuplets and I are here to say . . ."

"ONE! Always wear a—"

"That's Diane," said Mr. Sweetwine in a strangled voice.

"—lifejacket," finished Diane. She punctuated this advice with a toothy grin.

"TWO!" cried Lianne, popping into view. "Don't stand up in a boat!"

"THREE! Kids—ask your parents before you go out on the water." That was Marianne, holding Fluffy in her arms.

Suzanne beamed. "FOUR! Don't overload a boat!"

Anne bounced up behind her. "FIVE! And if you *do* fall out of a boat, hang onto it and yell for help!"

The screen melted into a jostling Greek-chorus arrangement of quintuplets, who shouted, "Be safe on the water!"

My mother released a low moan into the silence.

My voice capped off the broadcast. "This has been a message from the prime minister's family. Thank you for listening."

That was all. The living room filled with a ringing silence.

After a moment, my mother said, "I'm speechless."

"Good, isn't it?" I said.

"Ms. Fandango," said my mother, "I'm so sorry you've been inconvenienced. We had no idea . . ."

Mr. Sweetwine finished his coffee in three big gulps and held out his cup to Mrs. Gummidge, who filled it.

"Nonsense," said Gloria Fandango. "No apologies. It's absolutely marvelous. Super."

Mr. Sweetwine's hand trembled, sloshing coffee into the saucer. "I beg your pardon?"

"I said it's terrific," repeated Ms. Fandango. "It opens up a whole world of possibilities."

"No, it doesn't," said my mother firmly.

Ms. Fandango turned on one self-confident heel and leveled a cool look at her.

"I'm sorry," said Mr. Sweetwine. "My wife is trying to say that any use of the Sweetwine quintuplets for publicity purposes is strictly out of the question."

"No," said my mother. "Darling. That's not what I was trying to say."

"Although true," I supplied. "At least until today."

"Yes," said my mother. "No. I mean . . ." She frowned at me. "I mean, I'm sorry you had to come all the way out here, Gloria, and I agree with you that it's an interesting tape, but I just couldn't allow it to be aired."

"Why *not?*" I demanded.

"Ah-hum," said Mr. Sweetwine.

"Jordan?" My mother fixed him with a look. "You mean you think they should be allowed to air it?"

"I didn't say that," said Mr. Sweetwine.

Everyone started to speak at once.

"Why *not?*" I demanded again. "Excuse me? Hello? Why *not?*"

"Excuse me!" Gloria Fandango called out over the babble. "Pardon me. If I could . . . if I could have your—"

"—attention!" I cried helpfully.

". . . your attention," she echoed. "I do *not* intend to air this tape."

Dead silence.

"Why *not?*" I yelled for the fourth time.

"Of course, it's very interesting," she said, "but we had something more . . . something else in mind."

All eyes were on her.

"I'd like to do a documentary," she said.

"A documentary," echoed Mr. Sweetwine.

"Making your family—with your permission and your help, Prime Minister—the focus for a show about how Canadian families adapt to remarriage."

"Oh dear," said my mother.

"Our family as . . . ." Mr. Sweetwine pondered this, ". . . our family as the *focus.*"

"An example to the nation, if you will, sir."

The man in the business suit coughed and reached quickly for his coffee.

"I see," said Mr. Sweetwine. "Yes, I see. An example."

"We thought it would be a good idea," Gloria Fandango went on, "to get some footage of your new family celebrating its first Canada Day together."

"Oh. Mm-hm." Mr. Sweetwine bobbed his head like a nodding dog in the back window of a car.

"As you are probably aware," she continued, "the city is planning a balloon race as part of the celebrations this year."

"A balloon race . . ." echoed Mr. Sweetwine, glancing over at the man in the suit, who nodded.

"Hot air balloons," said Ms. Fandango. "Two dozen or more. To be launched from Parliament Hill. If the conditions are favorable, they will travel downriver, sir. We were thinking of the wonderful footage we might get as the balloons pass the foot of your garden. Footage of the quin . . . the children . . . watching the flypast."

My stepfather's face had actually begun to glow with this shared vision.

"We believe our viewers would be inspired and moved by the opportunity to share, if you will, those moments with you and your family, sir." Ms. Fandango lowered her eyes. "And with the election coming up next fall . . . well, I'm sure you'll agree that it's never too soon to lay the foundations for a successful campaign."

I held my breath. A single word might break the spell.

"Jordan," said my mother, but it was clear that the idea was taking shape in the prime minister's mind. He lifted his gaze and fixed it on what might have been a hot-air balloon rising in the distance had it not been Gloria Fandango's beautifully coiffed head. His brow cleared. His expression became practically noble. His voice rang with authority and vision.

"Well, now," he said. My mother surrendered her protests. The prime minister had spoken.

❦ ❦ ❦

Mrs. Gummidge started calling it "this fiasco."

"I'm going to be expected to perform miracles in aid of this fiasco," she said. "Mark my words, nothing good can come out of this fiasco."

"Mr. Sweetwine," she said, "will waste no time summoning me to discuss this fiasco."

She was right. The summons came the very next evening after dinner.

"My compliments," said Mr. Sweetwine, "on tonight's splendid meal."

Mrs. Gummidge said, "Thank you," stiffly. She says the prime minister has a powerful way of studying a person, and over the years she has had to stand up many times under that gaze, which almost always leads to a request for *cochon de lait, farci à la trébizonde*. So she stood tall with all her strength.

"Mrs. Gummidge," he said, "I know I can count on you to be the very soul of discretion. CBC television has decided to produce a one-hour documentary about this family."

Obviously, Gummy already knew this. It was all part of a game the Sweetwines were used to playing—it should have been called "Household Staff are Blind and Deaf when Things Happen to the Family in their Presence."

Mrs. Gummidge just widened her eyes to show she was interested.

"Gloria Fandango felt it might be a good idea to film the central scene around a family dinner," he went on. "The meal would be a focal point. A highlight, if you will."

Mrs. Gummidge raised both eyebrows as he flashed a smile of powerful dimensions. "Would you be so kind as to oversee the barbecuing of said repast?"

Mrs. Gummidge's eyebrows were beginning to disappear into her hairline. She cleared her throat. "Barbecuing, sir?"

"I'm sure the children will enjoy it," he said, "and if the weather is good . . . and since the hot air balloons will be passing the back garden . . ."

"I see, sir," said Mrs. Gummidge. "And if I might ask, sir, whether you would like me to prepare a . . . another dinner in case of something unforeseen?" She had been about to say "a proper dinner," which wouldn't have done at all. "A sort of . . . indoor one, sir?"

"Not necessary, Mrs. Gummidge. The grounds staff will erect a tent in case of inclement weather."

This time, Mrs. Gummidge couldn't help widening her eyes. She says the idea of all of us stampeding around hot coals in the rain nearly took her breath away.

"Very well, sir," she said.

Mr. Sweetwine opened and closed his fountain pen about a dozen times.

"Was there something else, sir?"

He glanced up like a boy with a guilty secret.

"Well," he said, "if you could . . . ha-ha . . . make it look as if we do this . . . well . . . often."

"Oh," said Mrs. Gummidge. "Sir?"

"The fact is," he confessed, "since the CBC wants to set us up as a model for the ordinary family, I'd like to create a bit of a good impression. You know. Regular father-type and all. If you see what I mean?" He cleared his throat and chuckled nervously. "I'm sure everything will go just swimmingly."

The lid of his pen flicked across the table and bounced off the far wall with a clatter. He cleared his throat again.

"Yes, sir," said Mrs. Gummidge. "Just swimmingly."

Chapter 22

Sid was smiling down at me. He had the nicest brown eyes I'd ever seen. When I looked up from the wicker chair in the sun room, where I'd been daydreaming, and found him grinning at me, my heart did a backflip and started bumping crazily against my ribs.

"Let me get this straight," I said. "You want to lock us in the pantry?"

He laughed. His teeth were very white and straight.

"It's a security drill," he said. "Extra precautions for the Canada Day thing."

"You want to lock us in the *pantry,*" I repeated, trying to make him smile again, but he didn't.

"Come on," he said. "The rest of them are already in the kitchen."

They were. The quintuplets were there, poking each other and giggling. My mother was there, tapping her finger against the corner of her mouth, looking uneasy. Mr. Sweetwine was leaning against the refrigerator, droning into a cordless phone. Mrs. Gummidge and the other kitchen staff were there. When Sid and I came down the corridor from the front hall, I felt as if I were walking onto a stage.

"There we go," said Sid. Something in his manner had changed. He crouched down like a football player and put his hands on his knees. He talked to us as if we were little children.

"Let's play a game," he said. "All right?"

We gaped at him. Marianne slid me a sideways look, and I had to swallow a snort of laughter. From the sidelines, my mother fired me a warning glance, and Mrs. Gummidge tried to slay me with her eyes.

"But this is a very serious game," Sid went on. "And if we ever have to play it for real, I need to know I can count on you. Every one of you. Okay?"

Anne folded her lips between her teeth and bit them to keep from laughing. She crossed her arms and hugged herself.

Someone had to answer him, but we were all so close to hysterics that no one dared open her mouth. The silence lengthened, and Sid pulled nervously at his ear.

"Okay," said Lianne in a high strained voice. It was terrible. All six of us dissolved into helpless laughter. The quints absolutely howled. I laughed, too, but then I saw the way Sid glanced back at my mother and Mrs. Gummidge. A couple of the kitchen staff slid their hands over their mouths to hide their grins, but my mother and Gummy wore matching expressions of weariness and impatience. Mr. Sweetwine put his finger in his ear and talked more loudly into the phone. Sid chewed his lip. He wanted to impress them, and we were making him look bad.

Suddenly, I didn't feel like laughing anymore. I stopped, glared at my stepsisters, and said, "Shut up, you guys. Shut up."

One by one, they stopped laughing and fixed puzzled gazes on me. My mother exchanged a mystified glance with Gummy.

"Okay," I said to Sid. "Go ahead."

He shot me a grateful look that made me go all mushy, and I had to look away.

"So this is the game," he said. "When I say 'Security Drill,' I want you to run into the pantry as fast as you can. And when you're all in there I'm going to slam the door and lock it. Okay?"

"Why?" demanded Marianne.

"Because the pantry is the safest place in the house. No windows, see?"

We peeked in. He was right. There were no windows.

"And a good sturdy lock on the door," he continued, "which only the security staff can open. Oh, and Mrs. Gummidge, of course, so she can prepare your dinners."

Everybody snickered at this little joke.

"Security drill!" said Sid, suddenly. We scrambled into the pantry. He slammed the door, the key turned in the lock, and we stood there looking at each other among all the cans and boxes, tubs and jars and bags of food. Then Sid opened the door and let us out again.

"There," he said in a breezy way. "Good work! That wasn't so bad, was it?"

We shook our heads and agreed that no, it was not bad, it was really nothing at all. I flicked a glance at my mother and had the distinct impression that she was trying not to grin. I scowled at her.

"So if I ever come up to you and say 'Security Drill,' no matter what you're doing, I want you to stop immediately and run into the pantry. As fast as you can. All right?"

"Sure," I said. "How come we're learning this now?"

"Yeah," said Anne. "We never had to before."

"Hey," Sid answered with another dazzling smile, "you've got a new guy on your security staff. What can I say?"

My mother crossed her arms.

"About the situation on July the first," she said.

"Yes," said Sid. "We'll be running extra ground patrols on that day. For one thing, there will be television crews coming and going and, well, we'd just like to make sure we're covered. And of course we'll have to shut down our helicopter patrols for a couple of hours."

"Really," said my mother.

"Well, yes," he said. "We can't deploy a chopper anywhere near the hot air balloons. The wash from the rotors would be disastrous."

"Mm-hm," my mother said. "Well, you know you can count on our girls not to give you any trouble. Right, ladies?"

We all said that Sid could definitely count on us, and everybody started making restless movements as if they were ready to leave the kitchen. Mr. Sweetwine was still talking on the cordless phone. As the others began to drift away, I felt a big hand close around my shoulder, and when I looked into Sid's smile, I felt my knees go wobbly.

"I want to thank you," he said, "for making your sisters pay attention. This is important stuff, and I'm really glad to have some help from someone as smart as you."

If I were a bird I would have opened my beak wide and started singing madly at the top of my lungs.

"That's okay," I said. The words tripped over themselves.

"And you know what else? I'm going to find out who was black-mailing Nick and Nanny."

He stopped, looked at me keenly with brown eyes that made it hard to think, and said, "Are you? How are you going to do that?"

"Detective work," I said. "Clues and stuff." I hoped he wouldn't ask for details.

He didn't. He eased his serious face into a charming smile and said, "Good for you. And if you find out anything, will you promise to tell me? We could work together on it."

My heart flew up. If it got out of my body it would go bumping around the ceiling. I couldn't seem to make my mouth work. I just jammed my hands into my back pockets and nodded vigorously. Sid nodded back and started to usher me out of the kitchen.

We started down the kitchen corridor, but before the others could disperse, Sid clapped his hands and shouted, "Security Drill!"

Marianne and Diane, who had made it as far as Gummy's sitting room, stared at him in surprise.

"You *guys!*" I called in an exasperated voice as I dashed back to the pantry. I was the first one to cross the threshold. I glanced back. Sid fixed me in the powerful beam of his smile. Then the others caught on and ran into the pantry, and the door slammed shut and the key turned in the lock.

We stood looking at each other.

"This is stupid," said Anne.

"No, it's not," I replied. The others turned away to examine the pantry shelves.

"I wonder if we could eat a whole jar of peanut butter before he opens the door," said Lianne, but before we could even get the lid off, the door was swinging open and Sid was saying my name.

"What?" I answered.

"Telephone," he said with a crooked smile. "Good work. I mean it."

I grinned back at him, and my heart went skipping along the corridor ahead of me.

The phone call was from my father. He asked how I was, and when I told him I'd been hiding out in the pantry with the quintuplets, he was appalled.

"Why do they make you do that?" he demanded.

"I don't know," I said. "Security. In case of terrorists or kidnappers or . . . I don't know. Hijackers or something."

"Not hijackers," he said.

"I guess not."

"I shudder to think that the world has come to this," he said. "I really do."

"It's okay," I said.

"I shudder to think that this is the new life your mother wanted for you."

"Dad . . ."

"Never mind, then," he said with a sigh. "Tell me what fun things you're doing these days."

I told him about the upcoming barbecue and the Canada Day balloon race and Gloria Fandango's documentary and how Mrs. Gummidge kept calling the whole thing "this fiasco." I told him about the menu and the staffing and the elaborate preparations. I was just about to describe our latest game, which was "Territorial Waters," when he interrupted me.

"When did you say this fiasco would be taking place?"

I told him July first, but it didn't satisfy him. He wanted to know the time and who was organizing the balloon race and what exactly Gloria Fandango wanted to do. Then he asked another question and another, and before I knew it I was repeating everything I had already told him, detail by detail, flattered by his sincere interest and the way he wanted to know absolutely everything. I loved the way he laughed.

I was just about to describe "Territorial Waters" when he humphed and interrupted me again. "Oops, Willie. Here comes Mrs. Silverman for the centerpieces. Her party's tomorrow. I must go. Talk to you soon, love."

And he was gone.

I set down the receiver carefully and sat with my hands on my knees, feeling annoyed and affectionate and very, very worried all at the same time.

Chapter 23

"I want to talk to you about your father," said my mother. She swooped up the path toward me so unexpectedly that I jumped. She put her hand on my shoulder and sat down on the step beside me.

I had been sitting outside the servants' entrance, near the cedar hedge, remembering the sound of the bell on the door of my father's flower shop and the cool quiet of the city garden after a busy Saturday morning serving customers.

"These postcards," she said. "There are hundreds of them. A hundred each day, darling, and I don't see how your father manages to write them *and* run the shop. Unless, maybe, someone is helping him?"

"Maybe he photocopies them?" This came out like a gasp. A lot of little somethings stampeded in my stomach. I hugged my knees tightly.

"You said yourself that wouldn't work, darling." She was troubled and beautiful. "Look at these postcards. Here. The security staff have identified seven different kinds of handwriting. This one is your father's. Do you recognize any of the others?"

"No." I gulped.

"Are you sure, darling?"

"Yes." There were birds in my chest beating wildly to get out.

"But there's something else," she went on. "Do you see the cancellation mark on this stamp? That postcard is from your father. Now look at this one."

"What's wrong with it?"

"It's been marked on with a felt pen. It hasn't gone through the post."

"Maybe they just missed it. Maybe the machine broke down and they had to do it by hand."

"But it's the same with all the others, except the few in your father's handwriting. And do you notice he's the only one who used postage stamps? All the others have Christmas seals instead of stamps."

"Oh," I said. "Rats."

"Where did you get the postcards, Willa?"

"With the last bunch of books he sent." Something terrible was happening. A big lump was growing underneath the panicky birds inside me, forcing them into my throat. "He didn't *ask* us to," I said in a rush. "It was me. It was my fault."

"Us? Did you make the quintuplets help?"

"No." At the look on her face I said, *"No"* again, more firmly, and looked away. "They wanted to. They thought it was . . ."

"They thought it was what?"

"Funny," I mumbled into my knees.

"Do *you* think it's funny?"

"No." It wasn't funny at all. It was horrible.

"Oh, Willa," she said in a broken voice.

"What?"

"Do you miss your father that much?"

"What do you think?"

"Do you miss him so much you'd go to such lengths to hurt me? And you'd even get the quints to help you?" She was almost crying.

I wanted to answer, "Yes! Yes, I miss him!" but everything would have shattered inside me. I didn't say anything.

My mother laughed hollowly. It came out like a sob. "What a lot of work. All those postcards," she said. "And you got each of the quints to write twenty, every day for three weeks? They must be very devoted to you."

"I'm teaching them about the real world," I mumbled.

She laughed again. Then she sat there for a long time with tears shining on her eyelashes and shook her head.

"I wanted so much for you to love it here." She breathed the spring air and gazed over the wide river to the Gatineau Hills beyond. "And you seem to like the quints well enough. Don't you?"

"They're okay. It's not that."

"Then what is it, darling? Please tell me."

"I keep thinking of the shop. And the flat. And the back garden."

"Oh, Willa." She released a breathy little laugh into the morning air. "That was more than three years ago! Every faucet in the place dripped. All the drains were clogged. Snow used to come through the cracks in the bathroom window. There were roaches. Don't you remember?"

I didn't answer.

She laughed again. This time there were hard edges to her laughter. "We were living like *squatters*—struggling to make ends meet, working morning until night. It was no life for you. I owed you something better than that."

"Remember those two big fridges full of flowers?" I asked. "Remember when it rained, and Dad used to let me roll the awning over those pails of flowers on the sidewalk? And when the sun came out there would be little sparkles of rain on all the petals?"

"Sweetheart, that happened once. Twice, at the most. And you couldn't have been more than seven." She was close to exasperation. "The rest of the time it was bugs and leaky pipes and peeling wallpaper. You don't understand, darling. I couldn't let you live like that."

"There were birds in the back yard," I said.

"There are birds *here*," my mother protested. As if on cue, a robin in the cedar hedge opened its throat and poured a song into the garden.

I couldn't speak. I hugged myself tighter than ever.

"What is this really about, Willa?" she asked.

My heart squeezed so hard I thought I would have a heart attack.

"He says he'll change," I said finally. "If he could just have a chance. Just one more chance."

"We've talked about this a hundred times," she said. "Willa, listen to me. He is not going to change."

"He says he will!"

"It's because of the wedding. Don't you see that? Don't you

wonder why he hasn't tried to get me back before this? Not once in three whole years?"

I pulled so hard on my shoelace that the plastic tip came off. My mother ran a weary hand down the side of her face.

"There's another thing," she said.

I pulled the tip off the other shoelace.

"I love your stepfather," she said.

I didn't reply.

"I'm married to your stepfather," she said.

I curled my fingers into hard balls. I curled my arms around my knees and held myself tightly together.

"If you wanted to try again with Dad," I said in a strangled voice, "maybe it could work out."

"No," she said. "I love Jordan. And I love you."

"Don't say that," I said. "Dad's all alone there, trying to run the shop. All by himself."

There was a painful pause.

"You really like it here," I said after a moment. She got that weary look on her face, the one she used to get when she saw the laundry hamper full of dirty clothes.

"Yes," she said cautiously.

"Why?"

She just looked at me.

"Really," I said. "I'm not starting a fight or anything. I really want to know."

"Willa," she said. "We are living in this absolutely gorgeous house with five fabulous little girls whose father loves us all very much."

"He doesn't love me," I said.

"Don't be ridiculous. Of course he does."

"He doesn't. He doesn't even know me." I caught the dirty-laundry look again and added, "I'm not trying to pick a fight."

"Of course not," she said, but her voice stung.

"You've got all new clothes," I said, "and a new car, a new house, new furniture, new friends. New daughters, even. Everything."

She narrowed her eyes. "I'd better not hear what I think I'm hearing. If you *dare* to suggest I married Jordan for material gain . . ."

That shocked even me. For a second, I forgot what I'd been

going to say. I just looked at the angry blue eyes burning in her lovely face.

"You mean for his money?" I croaked. "No."

She relented. "I'm sorry. What were you getting at?"

"I guess you hated the way things were with Dad. I guess you hated everything about it."

"I hated a lot of it." She sighed and brushed the hair from her forehead. "Not all. I don't know. It isn't that simple."

I sat looking down at my fingers. My nails were bitten short. My knuckles were red and rough—not like the smooth clean hands of the quintuplets.

"It seems like I'm the only thing in your life that's left over from the old days," I said. "If I went and lived with Dad, you could just forget about all of it—you know, make a fresh start."

She stared at me as if I were a rat in a laboratory maze. She looked like someone who had never met me before.

"Willa," she said slowly, "what on earth have you been thinking?"

I shrugged. "If I went to live with Dad, you'd end up with the kind of family you've always wanted."

"Do you think I *want* you to go live with Howard? Is that what you think? In spite of everything I've said?"

My voice was thin and high, squeezing painfully in my throat. "Then your new family would be . . . would be . . . clean," I said, "and nice. The way you like it."

"Clean and *nice?*"

"You know," I said helplessly. Hot tears burned my eyelids and I blinked furiously to hold them back.

She choked on a laugh and grabbed me by the shoulders. "No, I *don't* know, you ridiculous child. Come here." She hugged me and rubbed the back of my head, hard, so all my hair stood up. Then she sobbed again and gave me a little shake. "Clean and *nice?* What is that supposed to mean?"

"Like them," I said. "The quints. I know that's what you want, but I can't be like them. I just don't know how."

That did it. The sobs just burst out of me, and I howled as I hadn't howled since the day we arrived at the official residence.

"Do you want to go back to your father for a while?" The words came out as if someone were tearing them from her. I wiped my eyes with the palms of my hands and drew a shuddering breath. My heart thudded against my knees. I stared hard at Wilton Amaryllis's muddy rake, which he'd left beside the door.

"Yes," I said.

The silence tightened around us. The air seemed to hold its breath. The yard waited. I felt as if an earthquake were about to split it in half.

"How long would you stay?" she asked in a strained voice. She was crying, too. She wiped the tears away with the side of her finger.

"A week," I said.

She let out a shaky breath, as though she'd been expecting something much worse. She smoothed the skirt over her knees with a soft rustle of silk. She sat still for a long moment, sniffling.

"Pack your things," she said. "I'll go talk to Jordan. This time nobody will stop you from visiting your dad."

❦ ❦ ❦

She put her foot down with Mr. Sweetwine. I heard his voice booming around the library and her voice answering insistently, droningly, like a bumblebee, on and on, never tipping over into anger.

". . . don't want it to look as if she doesn't like it here. We can't afford another scandal . . . election in the offing . . . you must be able to see that . . ."

She answered calmly, quietly, confidently.

"Just for a week," she said.

The words were not important. I could tell just from the tone of her voice that no matter what he said, it wouldn't make any difference. My mother had made up her mind.

I sat on the bottom step of the spiral staircase, hugging my knees, and wondered why my feelings were clambering and tumbling all over themselves in such a nonsensical way.

When my mother swept out of the library, closed the door neatly behind her, and nodded at me, there was a tiny encouraging smile on her lips. My feelings rose, like a swarm of bees, and circled around and around.

"Pack up your things," she said. "Everything's all right."

Chapter 24

My father's shop was on a little street crammed with bakeries, bookstores, and delicatessens in a shabby corner of the city that had been there forever. The shop used to be a house. Now the ground-floor rooms were jammed with houseplants, greenery, buckets of bouquets, and display cases. The smell of damp earth, wood rot, and flowers filled the shop and spilled into the street.

My mother drove me there herself. Mr. Sweetwine made us take along bodyguards—one for each of us. I chose Sid, who came with another guard in the car with us, but my mother made them sit in the back seat, where they looked out the window in a bored way like two sulking boys.

When we arrived, my father was with a customer. He stood under the green and white awning between two pails of roses. The customer was an old man, who stared when my father stopped talking in midsentence. Dad approached the car in a daze.

I dragged my suitcase from the front seat. Sid got out, too, and leaned against the car with his arms crossed.

"I'll pick you up on Saturday afternoon, Willa," my mother said from the driver's seat. With the other bodyguard still in the back of the car, she looked like a chauffeur or a taxi driver. She smiled at my father in a funny way. He dropped an arm-load of roses on the sidewalk and stood gawking at us.

"Louise," he said.

"Howard." My mother nodded. I thought she was going to drive away without another word, but she seemed to change her mind. She tightened her grip on the steering wheel. Her cheeks were very pink. "I'll pick her up on Saturday afternoon."

"Oh," said my father. "Okay. How are you?"

"Perfect. Thank you. If you don't mind, before I leave Willa here, this security officer would like to check the alarms and locks you installed."

Cars were honking. She waved the other drivers away impatiently. My father stood staring at her with his mouth half-open.

"Howard, please," she said.

"Go ahead." His voice was numb and distant. Sid strode past him into the flower shop while the customer continued to stare, and I shifted my suitcase from one hand to the other.

The silence lengthened.

"I saw that article about the fund-raising dinner," my father said.

"Oh," my mother replied distantly. "Yes, it was quite a success."

I think she was relieved when Sid came back, opened the passenger door, and got out his overnight bag. He reminded me of a little kid going to his first sleep over. I wondered if he had packed his red Mountie uniform, and if he had, where he was keeping his hat.

"The security is satisfactory," he said.

"See you on Saturday, Willa," said my mother. "Good-bye, Howard." When she was gone, my father put his head down and started back toward the place where the customer was waiting.

"Dad." There was a frog in my throat. I grabbed my suitcase and followed him. "I'm here."

That seemed to wake him up. He put one arm around me, kissed the top of my head, and said, "You're here, Willie. We're going to have a nice time together." Then he let me go. He scooped the roses from the sidewalk and went into the shop without another word.

❁ ❁ ❁

It wasn't exactly the way I'd thought it would be. My bed behind the screen in the living room was narrower and lumpier than I remembered. The kitchen was grayer. The sounds of traffic and sirens kept waking me up at night. It was hot, and my father was busy. When he wasn't busy with customers, he was busy making flower arrangements or working on his accounts. And when he wasn't busy with the shop, he was inventing things.

He used to tell my mother and me that someday he would create one thing—one magical invention—that people had always needed but never *knew* they needed. Then we would be rich, and every morning we would have leisurely breakfasts in the garden and take long walks on the mountain and eat scrumptious dinners in French restaurants overlooking the water.

Of course, these things never happened. I stood in the stuffy living room and thought about them. Downstairs, the bell rang again and again as customers came into the shop. I should have gone to help, but instead I ran down the backstairs, past Sid, who sat reading the newspaper at the kitchen table, and into the garden.

I missed my mother. At the same time, I felt guilty for missing her when everybody had made this effort for me to be with my dad. Then I felt guilty for feeling guilty because he was trying to run the shop and entertain me at the same time. And somehow the whole mess seemed to be my fault.

My father's shed sagged against a brick wall in the far corner of the garden. Inside the shed, I knew, were the remains of half-invented things: random-click cameras for taking candid self-portraits, musical kettles, self-cleaning goldfish bowls, electric coat hangers, and double-scent perfumes that smelled of daisies in the morning and gardenias at night. None of these things worked, of course. My mother said my father specialized in *starting* inventions.

I sat in the broken rocker beside the shed and smelled the shady smell of wet leaves. I felt as if I'd lost something, but I couldn't think what it was. Cars honked, tires squealed, and trucks roared past the front of the house. The city was full of life and energy, but I felt empty.

My father hurried past, going to fetch a fresh roll of wrapping paper from the shed. He wore that flyaway distracted look that meant there were several customers waiting to be served. I should have jumped up to help. I didn't. I sank deeper into the chair, hiding, as still as a cat.

I didn't think he had seen me. When he said, "Willie," I

jumped. My foot slipped off the seat of the chair into the damp grass.

"Yeah?" I said sheepishly.

"Have you been in the shed?"

He stood in the doorway, half-hidden by the plank door with its dangling padlock.

"No," I said. The shed was strictly off limits, and I knew it, and he knew I knew it. I'd never been inside without an invitation. When I used to live there with my parents, I would stand on the broken rocking chair and peer into the shed through the dusty window, but I hadn't done that for years. To tell you the truth, there had never been much to see in there—just a jumble of wires and bits of plastic, old jars full of hardware and scrap lumber.

"It looks . . . different," my father said. "You're sure you did-n't touch anything?"

"No, Dad. No."

Sometimes I have trouble sounding as innocent as I really am. My father didn't believe me. I could tell.

"Really," I insisted. "I don't even know where the key is."

He didn't say anything. He just locked the shed door, hefted the heavy roll of wrapping paper into his arms, and staggered back toward the shop.

When he was gone, I climbed up on the broken rocker and peered through the dusty window.

I received two shocks.

First, my head reached almost to the top of the window and gave me an awful feeling, like Alice in Wonderland, of having turned into a giant. The last time I had looked in the shed, I had been eight or nine years old, stretching high on my tiptoes, clinging to the windowsill with my fingernails. Now I had to duck down to keep from hitting my head on the frame.

The second shock was even worse. I expected, when my eyes adjusted to the shadows, to see the usual junk spilling from Dad's benches onto the old metal stool and even onto the cement floor. Instead, I saw a . . . well, a thing.

It was huge—a shapeless lump that nearly filled the shed, blocking most of the view through the window. It reached almost to the ceiling and touched the workbenches on either side. It was wrapped in shiny black garbage bags, tied haphaz-ardly with elastic cords and floral tape.

It scared me.

I climbed down from the rocking chair and looked up at the sill. Next year, if I wanted to, I'd probably be able to peek through the window without even climbing.

The sickening feeling of loss grew worse than ever.

I went into the kitchen.

"Sid," I said. "Did you go into my father's shed?"

He was turning the pages of a newspaper. He shook his head.

"No. Why?"

"Dad thinks someone might have been in there." There was an African violet on the drainboard. I poked my finger into the soil beneath its furry leaves. "Maybe you could check it out."

"I will," he said. "Thanks for telling me. You're very observant. Your dad must be proud of you."

He studied the paper.

"I've been thinking," I said, "about the blackmailer." He looked up again.

"Really," said Sid.

"Wilton told Nanny I stole a letter from her room." I fiddled with the violet. I tugged off its brown petals. "But I didn't."

"I believe you," he said.

This was such a relief that for several seconds I couldn't talk.

"But Wilton said one of the security guards saw me doing it."

"Really," said Sid.

"So maybe the guard is lying. Maybe you could talk to Wilton and find out who it was."

Sid smiled and glanced down at the newspaper.

"I'll tell you a secret," he said. "You're absolutely right. We've been investigating one of the security staff for several days. It looks like he might be the perpetrator."

My eyes widened.

"So, you see," he said, "you *would* make a great security officer. I hope you'll consider it seriously when you get old enough."

"Oh," I said in a croaking voice. "Yes, I will."

"Of course, we're not ready to release our findings yet," he said, "but I know I can count on you to keep this quiet. Right?"

"Oh. Yes," I repeated.

145

"Excellent," he said. He looked back down at the paper. I opened my mouth to say something, but there was a gaping emptiness where the words used to be. I closed my mouth. His hair was very black and curled across his forehead in a nice way. He was looking down, and his eyelashes brushed softly against his cheeks. I stood there, staring.

After a long moment, he shifted his eyes toward me. He waggled his eyebrows. I grinned. I wanted to dash around the backyard, jumping and yipping like an overexcited puppy. I did the next best thing. I fled.

That night, after a hurried dinner of hot dogs and potato chips, Sid went upstairs to watch TV and I sat on an upside-down bucket in the shop, snipping the stems of the new flowers and sorting them into plastic pails: carnations, glads, mums, pink roses, yellow roses, and long-stemmed red roses. At the counter, my father lettered a sign for tomorrow's specials. He stopped now and then to run his fingers through his thinning hair.

I wished I could make him laugh.

I told him how Mrs. Gummidge was trying to keep an eye on us while my mother interviewed replacement nannies.

I asked him, as I always did, what he was inventing these days. I expected him to say "self-baking potatoes," or "disappearing fingerpaint," or something as he always did, but there was a funny pause. He cleared his throat.

"It's that thing in your shed, isn't it?" I asked suddenly. "That big lump. That's what you're working on."

"Willie!" My father hardly ever got angry, but when he did it was like meteors flashing across a night sky. "You said you hadn't gone in the shed! How many times have I—"

"I didn't." I whacked a slice off the stem of a carnation. "I saw it through the shed window."

He didn't reply.

"At least you could tell me what it is," I persisted.

The meteors zipped off into the stratosphere. His voice mellowed. He capped his marking pen. After a moment, he looked up and laughed. His laughter was the best thing I had heard all day.

"You'll love it, Willie. I know you will," he said. "I've been taking lessons for weeks."

"What kind of lessons, Dad?"

146

He grinned.

"It's another big romantic gesture, isn't it?" I demanded. For once I didn't feel like giggling. I didn't know why, and I guess my father didn't either because there was another funny pause.

The next thing I knew, he was coming around the counter, settling himself on an old packing crate, pushing a much-folded brochure toward me, smiling encouragingly.

I opened the brochure. A bunch of irises slipped off my lap and scattered across the floor. My clippers tumbled into a can of water. I looked up sharply to see if my father was joking, but he wasn't. He winked at me.

"*Ballooning,* Dad?"

"Oh, Willie," he said. "It's the most wonderful . . . it's like nothing you've ever . . ."

I gulped.

"When you're up there," he said, "and you can see everything spread out below you and everything is so absolutely silent and still and . . . perfect . . . it's the best feeling in the whole . . . Why are you looking at me that way?"

"It's because of the balloon race, isn't it?"

He looked straight at me. Nobody else ever looked at me that way. Nobody else could make me feel I was such an interesting person.

"Won't that be something, Willie?" he asked. "All those balloons going up at the same time? Won't that be something to see?"

"Oh, Dad," I said.

He tilted his head. His glasses reflected the light from the fridges full of flowers, and I couldn't read his expression.

"I guess so," I said. "Sure it will. It sure will be something to see."

He picked up the flowers and put them back on my lap. He fished the clippers out of the water and shook them once or twice to dry them. I gave him back the brochure, which he folded carefully and tucked into his shirt pocket.

"I hope there won't be any trouble," I said, bending over my work. "I hope we won't be getting into any newspapers again."

My father laughed and picked up his marking pen, drumming a quirky little rhythm on the edge of the counter while he considered my words.

"Only trouble of the nicest kind," he promised. "The kind of trouble you and I enjoy the most." And he grinned that conspiratorial grin that always made me feel that no matter what happened, he and I were bound to share the fun of it. I felt the corners of my lips twitch upward, almost against my will. I grabbed the clippers and busied myself with my work.

🍁 🍁 🍁

The whole week was crazy. All day long, the bell was ringing, customers were asking questions, and we were busy, busy, busy eating sandwiches at the cash desk while my father worried about a late shipment of irises, the bouquets for the Reichertzes' anniversary party, and whether he was feeding me well enough.

We chatted over coffee at breakfast and drank tea before bedtime, but the days and nights were hollow, so the week became a thin corkscrew of something hard with emptiness both inside and outside. Sid sat all day reading the paper. In the evenings he watched the old black-and-white TV. He's my bodyguard, I said to myself. He's *my* bodyguard. But he didn't speak much. He didn't help at the counter or answer the phone. He seemed more like a statue than a person. I wondered what he would do if someone really tried to kidnap me. But of course no one did.

Then it was Saturday afternoon.

"Willie!" My father appeared at the back door. "I need a couple of rubber rings. Washers, maybe. No, tougher—a couple of slices of tubing. I think there's an old garden hose in the basement."

I hated going down to the basement. For one thing, I hate spiders. I hate the way they hide in corners and jump out at people. I tucked my neck down into the collar of my shirt and hurried as fast as I could. In a crate full of broken trellises, crumpled gardening gloves and trowels with dry earth still clinging to them, I found a garden hose attached to an old-fashioned sprinkler, the kind that used to stand like a stiff ballerina in the middle of the lawn, spinning crazily with outstretched arms. I remembered it from the days when we used to live here as a family. For a moment, when I wrestled it out of the box, everything seemed to smell of lilacs, and while I stood there in the damp basement, holding the sprinkler in both hands, I felt lightheaded as if I were floating in a slash of sunshine.

"Willie?" called my father.

I ran upstairs with the hose coiled over my shoulders. He was selling flowers to a bride and her mother. Two other customers waited patiently.

"Thanks, pet," said my father. "Be nice, will you, and run down to Theriault's for a bit of ribbon? It's Lavender Mist we want—the wide satin kind—about two meters."

I dropped the sprinkler and hose behind the cash desk and went. When I got back, the bride and her mother were still looking through the big sample book.

"Ta, my darling," said my father. "We've decided to go with Moonlight Roses after all, but thanks loads."

I went to sit on the back porch. The dizzy feeling of sun and lilacs came back, and I hugged my knees. The garden was a singing green, with geraniums, pansies, and marigolds shining like lights around its edges. The sprinkler turned lazily in the center, flinging water from its arms. The air shimmered wet and gold.

"I didn't need to cut the hose after all," said my father. He stood in the doorway behind me. "So Sid set it up and turned it on. Good little sprinkler, eh?"

"It's good," I agreed. All I could see was the sunlight shining through water, just as it had when we lived there as a family. When we were happy.

He lowered himself like an old man onto the step beside me. We sat watching the sprinkler as it turned around and around.

"It's been good to see you, Willie. Sorry things have been so hectic," he said.

"It's okay," I told him.

"You're happy there?" he asked. "Do they treat you well? Is it nice?"

There was a long pause while I tried to think of something to say. I don't know why it was so hard to answer him.

"It's good," I admitted finally. "It's okay. They don't let us out, though. Not even for school."

"Yes, I know," he said. "We'll see what we can do, eh, Willie? We'll think of a way to make things better. I'm glad you miss me, even a little."

As I listened to my father's kind voice, a great peace massed itself in the air above us. It hesitated, then spiraled down and drove itself into my heart.

I hugged him, and while I was hugging him my mother came through from the front of the shop. Sid hovered behind her in the dimness of the kitchen. I broke away from my father quickly. I was afraid to look up and see the pain in my mother's face, but her smile was firm and I thought she was truly happy to see me.

When she came upstairs to help me with my things, my heart twisted with gladness. She lifted my suitcase as if it didn't weigh anything and shook my father's hand with her slim gracious one. She smelled wonderful.

"Howard," she said, "I hope you both had a nice time." On the way down the stairs, her heels clicked deliciously. She shifted the suitcase to her other hand as the three of us emerged into the sunshine at the front of the shop. Sid was already swinging his overnight bag into the back seat of the car, where my mother's bodyguard was waiting. Sid flicked his fingers at me in a funny little greeting and grinned. The other guard didn't speak to him.

"Thanks for having her," my mother said.

"Don't thank me," said my father. "Don't ever thank me for that, will you?"

He hugged me once more and walked us to the car, where the security guards were already looking bored in the back seat. A customer was coming up the sidewalk toward the shop, but my father stepped around him and kept on walking with us. A shaky smile broke out on my face because, for a few seconds, my family was together there, the three of us, just the way I'd remembered it. Then I was in the car, reaching out the window toward my father. My fingers stretched wide like the wings of a butterfly, opening and closing as I waved good-bye.

"Well, good-bye for now," said my father. "Good-bye, Willie."

He turned grave eyes on my mother. "Louise?"

But she was already behind the steering wheel. She finished smoothing the skirt under her hips and closed the door. Two girls browsing in the window of the bakery next door turned to watch us. They wore sunglasses, and even though I couldn't see their eyes, I knew the exact moment they recognized us. They stopped and looked hard as if we were moving and talking in a show that was being put on just for them.

My mother didn't even glance at them. I suddenly realized

that this must happen to her—to my famous mother—all the time, out in the real world. As the girls whispered to each other and pointed, I fought back the urge to wave at them.

"Louise?" my father said again in an anxious voice.

"Please, Howard," she said tiredly, "don't start."

"But darling, I . . ."

"Good-bye, now."

She drove us smoothly out of the parking space, turned the corner, and adjusted her mirror. I didn't even have time to wave good-bye to my father. My heart was like an ice cube in my chest.

When she asked about my week, there wasn't much to tell. All the way home, neither of us mentioned a word about Dad.

Chapter 25

After a boring geography lesson on Friday afternoon, I went into my room, shut the door, and leaned my elbows on the sill, staring blindly down the driveway. My feelings whirled around and around like deerflies looking for a patch of skin to settle on. It had been that way for nearly a week, and no matter how many times I went over the situation I could not put it to rest.

My father's comments about the balloon lessons pestered me. When I slapped them away, they just circled back again. They got all mixed up with the swarm of minutes I'd spent that week at the flower shop, waiting for him to be less busy, and with one heavy thought of the mysterious lump which filled his shed, waiting. At the same time I remembered chatting with him over our chipped teacups and the way his whole face wrinkled with delight when I said something funny.

I wanted to tell my mother. But when I thought about confessing my worries, I knew with a burning certainty how she would act. She would mold her face into a reasonable professional mask as she listened to me, but inside she would be raging against my father. She would do a fine impression of a concerned listener, but underneath she would be busy inventing stinging things to say to Dad on the phone. Also, if I told her my suspicions, she would go straight to Mr. Sweetwine. And if Mr. Sweetwine found out about my father's plans, I could imagine only one result. He would fill the house with more Mounties and agents, sending some to Montreal to frighten and insult my father and putting more restrictions than ever on the quints.

Both of these options were so unbearable that I shook them off impatiently.

I couldn't think how to stop the idea that had gotten inside me and was starting to itch and swell. It wouldn't leave me alone, this worry that my father's latest caper was going to upset my mother and throw the household into a panic. And I couldn't, although I poked and squeezed and fussed over it, see why the idea didn't seem thrilling and hilarious to me. A few weeks ago it would have.

As I puzzled over these things, I watched the comings and goings of people in business suits who slid up and down the driveway in expensive cars, hurrying to and from their meetings with the prime minister. When they approached the front gate, Sid would come out of the gatehouse to check their identification. He charmed everyone with his big smile, but he didn't have much to do with the other guards. I wondered whether they were mean to him. When they laughed and chattered together, he stayed apart from them, doing his work. I remembered how he'd spent those days at my father's shop, staying away from us but watching everything from the back of the store, like a shadow. All week, he had observed us. He had taken in every detail.

Of all the people I could think of, he was the only one who would listen without jumping to conclusions and then, without fuss, do the best thing. That's how I made up my mind.

I must have approached the gatehouse more quietly than I thought because when I rapped on the door he jumped. His foot slipped off the edge of the wastebasket, tipping it with a clatter, and he snatched at his newspaper to keep it from falling into his lap. His brown eyes peered at me through the glass. They were like two wooden beads, unblinking. He wore the blank expression of someone who has been startled awake in an unfamiliar place.

He stirred and sat up. He flashed me the smile that always set my heart wheeling around inside my rib cage. He took a long look across the lawn at the house. Then he released the latch and let the guardhouse door swing open.

"Yes, Willa," he said.

"I need advice," I replied.

He looked toward the house again as though he thought someone might be watching him, possibly even laughing at him.

"It's great to see you," he said with another smile. My heart lodged itself in my throat. My ears got hot.

"Is there something I can do for you?" he asked.

I told him everything. It tumbled out like the Rideau Falls. I told him how lonely my father was and how busy and how he wanted my mother to love him better. I told him about my father's inventions and his big romantic gestures. I told him about the biggest romantic gesture of all, which my father had been planning for weeks, and how I thought I knew what it was and how it was going to upset everyone and how I didn't know what to do.

"You sound pretty worried," he said.

No one in the world understood me as well as Sid did. It was such a relief that I almost cried.

He listened with a kind of silent fascination as if he couldn't quite keep up with what I was saying. But he did listen. There was no doubt about that. I could practically see him ticking off details on a mental checklist, sorting them into columns. He was not just listening, either. He was remembering everything.

The conversation was a tremendous relief to me.

Not once did he interrupt to accuse me of overreacting or to tell me to get to the point or to say I must have misunderstood something. Not once did he laugh at me.

I told him more. I told him how harmless my father was and how bad it would be for everyone if he were to get arrested, especially on national television.

When I was done, my face was hot and I felt weak and empty.

"The thing is," I said, "can you figure out a way to keep him from getting into the balloon race? I mean, can you make it so he won't get close enough to be on the news?"

Sid looked up at the house again. He looked down at his logbook. Then he fixed me with a solemn stare.

"Yes," he said. "I'm proud of you for coming to me with this. You made a very mature decision—I know it wasn't easy."

I gulped and grinned foolishly. I said, "But can you do it quietly, so nobody has to know? I mean, even Mr. Sweetwine and my mother? So my father won't get into trouble?"

He looked at me again with his powerful gaze. "You can count on me. But I've got to be able to count on you, too."

"Oh," I said. "You can. For sure."

"And I know I can count on you to come to me if your father tells you anything else about his plans."

"Sure," I said.

"Maybe you could even get me a bit more information," Sid suggested. "It would help a lot. For example, you could ask him what time he intends to launch the balloon, and where he'll be leaving his car. That type of thing."

I could be a girl sleuth. An official one. My foolish grin widened. Then I thought about my father. I stopped smiling.

"What are you going to do to him?" I asked.

"Well," said Sid, "that information is classified. I can't tell you how, but I promise I'll keep him from spoiling your party. And I promise to be discreet about it."

"Okay," I said. But I must have sounded skeptical because Sid added, "The only thing that would mess things up would be if you talked to anyone about this. You won't, will you?"

"No!" I said. It hurt me that he would even think such a thing. I said again, "No, I won't!"

His brown eyes crinkled into the nicest smile, and he closed his hand on my shoulder. "I knew I could count on you."

I shoved my hands into my back pockets. I couldn't figure out how he was going to manage it, but he seemed completely confident. Besides, his black hair curled across his forehead in a way that made him look like a movie star.

"Don't worry," he said again. "I'll take care of it."

"Thanks," I said and fled.

That night, I slept more soundly than I had in all the weeks since my mother's wedding.

❦ ❦ ❦

Meanwhile, the quints laughed and quarrelled and planned strategies for the "Territorial Waters" game. We had given up "Endangered Species" soon after our near-fatal boating accident. To Mrs. Gummidge, "Territorial Waters" was just a lot of shouting and jumping on the furniture, which was the last thing she needed in her role as substitute nanny. She would stand on the steps outside the sun room and holler, "That's enough hullaballoo, now! Thank you all very much!" But I would not have used the word *hullaballoo* to describe "Territorial Waters," which was all about teamwork and boundary disputes.

I guess I don't blame Mrs. Gummidge for grumbling. In the midst of "Territorial Waters" and being in charge of the six of us, she was fussing day and night about the fiasco. If you have ever prepared for a nationally televised barbecue while supervising quintuplets, you will understand that the official residence was not its usual serene and elegant self.

The barbecue was shaping up to be a dizzy affair. Somewhere between Mr. Sweetwine's request for a simple family barbecue and the arrival of the television crews, things had gotten a bit out of hand. Never one to do things by half-measures, Gummy had surpassed herself with the preparations. *Cuisine Canada* had heard about the event and was going to do a photodocumentary about the meal, and she was more excited about it than she was about Gloria Fandango's project. Gummy said crystal punch bowls and mountains of potato salad thundered through her dreams, all shot through with lightning bolts of quintuplet mischief under the distant storm clouds of an approaching election. Still, none of us was prepared for what actually happened.

Chapter 26

As soon as Gloria Fandango stepped onto the velvety lawn, a string trio began to play breezy tunes under the awning. The bartender, with a flourish, poured something sparkly out of a bottle. A *Cuisine Canada* reporter scribbled notes and snapped photographs. Flowers nodded in the breeze, and the quints' voices rose in a clamor. They spilled from the sunroom, and even the great Gloria Fandango stopped and stared when they appeared, squabbling and laughing. My mother, cool and lovely in green silk, came forward and extended her hand. Mr. Sweetwine waved heartily from his position beside the roast pig.

"All this . . ." Ms. Fandango managed at last, stepping back as a technician hurried past with a coil of wire. "Well, it's not what I expected."

Since the game of the week was "Territorial Waters," the east side of the lawn belonged to Anne, and she patrolled it vigilantly. She had actually drawn up a treaty to allow the roasting of the pig to take place in this restricted area. Meanwhile, the west side, with its high cedar hedges, was under the joint jurisdiction of Lianne and Suzanne, who cruised up and down, protecting it from intrusion by any unauthorized vessels.

The quints were engaged in yet another boundary dispute, advancing and retreating, bumping into each other and shouting things like "Prepare to be boarded!" "Coast Guard! Coast Guard!" and "Throw me a line!"

The staff were used to this sort of thing. As they ferried back and forth between the kitchen and the picnic table, they merely stepped around the quints. But Gloria Fandango stared.

Mr. Sweetwine came forward with the basting brush in his hand. My mother made some gracious and intelligent remarks, and everyone laughed pleasantly. There was a lot of discussion about how the meal would proceed, what time the balloons would first appear, where the quints should stand to watch the flypast, and so on. Technicians hurried here and there, writing things on clipboards and tinkering with electrical equipment.

As for me, I got busy settling the boundary dispute, playing the parts of the Coast Guard, the provincial and federal governments, and two special interest groups, all at the same time.

That day, even more than usual, my radar was busily sweeping around and around as it tried to pick up traces of Sid. Last week I had told him all my father's plans—what time Dad was planning to launch the balloon, where he planned to park his car, and so on.

But afterward, I worried that I had betrayed my father. Then I worried that he might crash his balloon or upset my mother or get arrested. After that, I worried that he might do something unpredictable—something even Sid could not prevent.

🍁 🍁 🍁

I pressed my face against the railings. I clung so tightly to the fence that the skin stretched across my knuckles. I strained to hear what people on the boats were saying and sniffed the smoke from a dozen barbecues as they cooked their dinners and waited for the flypast to start.

I peered upriver so intently that my eyes blurred. I blinked and watched harder.

Bright dots of color had begun to rise into the clear sky. There was no doubt about it. The race had started. Balloons were sprinkled above the parliament buildings like a handful of confetti.

"There they go!" I yelled.

Everybody rushed to the fence: the quints, my mother, Mr. Sweetwine and Gloria Fandango . . . even the kitchen staff came running.

Down on the river, people cheered and hooted. A band began to play the national anthem. Someone whistled piercingly. My heart beat hard and fast as the balloons continued to go up—slowly, slowly. There were dozens of them. Every time I thought they'd all been launched, more would appear from behind the Parliament Hill. They traced long graceful curves out over the river.

Gloria Fandango was thrilled. She kept snapping her fingers at camera operators, flapping her hand to draw their attention to the best angles, pointing at the balloons and the spectators and Mr. Sweetwine in his barbecue apron. The quintuplets were all cute and adorable and identical, saying things like, "Ooo!" and "Look how beautiful!" and "Here they come!"

In the middle of the confusion, with the lights of four television cameras glaring behind us—at that moment when everyone's attention was riveted on the prime minister's family and every pair of eyes was fixed on the approaching balloons, I turned around to look for Sid.

That's when I saw it.

It was a rainbow-colored balloon. A strange balloon. A completely unexpected balloon.

It arrived too soon and too low. And it approached from an impossible angle—crossing against the wind, sneaking up behind us, coming from such an odd direction that I simply could not understand it.

It cruised above Sussex Drive, cleared the tops of the trees, and swooped down over the front lawn. I was so shocked that for a second I simply stood there. A gorgeous yellow banner, like a sash, enfolded the balloon's wicker basket. Big curly letters danced around it, spelling out PLEASE! LOUISE!

I squawked.

"Look!"

One technician and then another whirled and stared. Mrs. Gummidge turned and froze, opening and closing her mouth like a fish. It was my mother's scream that broke the spell.

"Howard?" she shrieked. "Is that you? Oh, my God!"

The man in the balloon saluted. My mother's screech, although it did not accessorize well with her silk suit and neat hair, did catch the attention of everyone in the area. Mr. Sweetwine jumped and staggered back. The startled quintuplets squealed. The kitchen staff fell away from the fence, jabbering and yelling.

"Roll the cameras!" bellowed Gloria Fandango, but the cameras were already rolling.

My father could not have hoped for a more dramatic entrance. He floated like an angel of the heavenly host, smiling down from his basket, while the late afternoon sun shone gold on his balloon and pandemonium broke out on the ground.

Sirens and alarms began to squall, but my father did not panic. He simply reached up to adjust a lever, which opened a valve, which let out an alarming hiss. The balloon rose and turned in a startlingly unballoonlike way. It shifted its weight until it groaned, like a very large person manoeuvring down the aisle of a crowded theater.

"It's my self-propelling mechanism, Willie!" he cried happily. "It's never been done before! Look! I can steer this thing anywhere I want!"

To prove it, he turned another lever. The balloon bellied eastward and sashayed over the treetops, flapping its yellow banner.

"Dad!" I yelled. "Go away! If they catch you, they'll . . ."

But he steered for the backyard, smiling. He seemed not to care about the security agents with their guns and loudhailers, who swarmed onto the lawn, chasing him.

"Get down! Get *down!*" someone roared, but we did not respond. The quintuplets were shrieking with excitement. Anne and Lianne had begun to sob with uncontrollable laughter. My mother kept screaming, "Don't shoot! Don't shoot him!"

"He's got something!" cried Suzanne. "It's a . . . box."

"What is it?" Marianne demanded. "What's he *doing?*"

"Get *down!*" yelled an exasperated Mountie.

But my father remained perfectly calm. He balanced the box on the edge of the basket, adjusted his glasses, and called, "Louise! My darling! I beg you to reconsider your decision. I offer you the dove of peace!"

Maybe you saw this on television. Later, the animal rights people accused him of throwing the cage, but I'm telling you he did no such thing. As he struggled to release the catch, the wire carrier slipped out of his hands, toppled over the edge of the basket, and plunged to the ground.

It was full of doves. Sometimes I think about how beautiful it would have been to see those white birds fly up toward the sun, against the jewel-like colors of my father's balloon. But it didn't happen that way.

You probably remember that sickening moment of impact—the burst of wings and feathers as the corner of the cage hit the ground and split open. The birds struggled to fly and everyone screamed and people kept yelling, "Get down. Get *down!*"

That would have been bad enough. But by this time, police cars were roaring around the side of the house, tearing muddy tracks into Wilton's lawn—into the territorial waters the quints had so recently been defending. Everything sparkled and flashed in the glare of police lights, and all around me there were guns and uniforms and terrified adults and panicked birds.

Still, I just stood there, gaping up at my father.

Then Sid broke free of the confusion and ran straight toward me.

🍁 🍁 🍁

"Security Drill," he panted. His voice was high, and his eyes—which were usually so icy and professional—bulged with excitement. "Security Drill! Now!"

The alarm continued to scream, drowning out everything else. Floodlights had snapped on, blasting everything with an unearthly shine. Mounties poured around the sides of the house and from every door. Security agents, in their dark suits, crisscrossed the yard, trying to yell over the shrieking alarm and the screams of the onlookers.

There was a roar so loud and unexpected that it sucked the breath right out of me. The rainbow-colored balloon skimmed the treetops and swooped back across the lawn. Everyone sprinted after it, arms and legs pumping.

"Go, Dad, go!" I hollered. "Go out over the river!"

I don't know if he heard me. Probably not. But he straightened his glasses and readjusted his self-propelling mechanism. It whirred and buzzed like a huge dragonfly, hurrying the balloon toward the river, trailing its wicker basket.

A strong hand grabbed my arm, spinning me around so sharply that I nearly fell.

It was Sid. His uniform shone eerily, nobly, in the glare of the floodlights. Behind him, Anne and Suzanne ran for the house, pausing to snatch at Marianne's hand, dragging her with them.

"Security Drill!" Sid shouted over the noise. "Didn't you hear me? Get the rest of the quints!"

161

Anne, Suzanne, and Marianne beat us to the sunroom door, but not by much. We were almost there when Diane tripped. I pressed my hand against a stitch in my side and paused to help her, but Sid had already scooped her up. He kept running, herding Lianne and me in front of him. I thought it was the most heroic thing I'd ever seen. He jerked open the sunroom door so hard that it crashed back against the side of the house.

"In here!" he ordered. We dashed through the sunroom, clattered down the hall, and exploded into the kitchen. Anne and Lianne were already in the pantry. Sid shepherded the rest of us toward them. He planted one hand on the small of my back, shoving me none too gently through the doorway. The key turned. We were alone.

It was stunningly quiet inside the windowless room, and none of us knew what to do. We were all gasping. Lianne and Anne leaned against the shelf where Mrs. Gummidge kept her homemade jams. Marianne nursed a sore wrist. Diane actually sobbed out loud, caught the rest of us looking at her, and stopped.

We hadn't been in the pantry for more than a minute or two when a key turned in the lock. The door swung inward, and we blinked at the man who shoved through it, blocking out the sunlight that streamed through the kitchen windows behind him.

I thought it was Sid, but it wasn't. It was someone big and paunchy in a plain gray jacket and jeans, and he was wearing a mask.

It was the mask that startled me more than anything else. It was the rubber kind, very realistic. Dark eyeballs glittered horribly. I screamed right out loud.

It was an Elvis Presley mask, and the man who wore it was pointing a gun.

He didn't speak. Marianne let out a cry that was more angry than frightened, but Diane cut loose with another of those heart-wrenching sobs, and I screamed again.

That's when I realized something was wrong. The man in the mask was forcing one quintuplet after another through the kitchen corridor, across the step, and through the rear door of Sid's waiting van. And instead of stopping him, Sid was *helping*.

I did not see how the man in the mask could be a security officer. He was nervous and twitchy, breathing hard as he pushed Anne forward and waggled the gun at Suzanne. Sid lifted Anne into the van and turned to do the same to Suzanne, but I just clung to the screen door, looking first at the man in the mask and then at Sid, struggling to understand.

"Don't stand there staring," Sid panted. "Get in the van. Quick!"

But it felt wrong.

He was reaching out to grab me, saying, "Let go of the door. Let go!" as he hoisted me off my feet and swung me toward the back of his van, where the scared quintuplets huddled.

"Hey!" I roared. "Hey!"

He uttered one of the few black curses that were *not* in my repertoire and tried to get his big hand over my face to shut me up.

I was still struggling and kicking when Mrs. Gummidge steamed around the corner of the house, saw Sid wrestling with me, opened her eyes wide and trumpeted, "Let them go!" in a voice like a foghorn.

I was so surprised, I let go of the door. Sid threw me into the van.

"What are you doing?" bellowed Mrs. Gummidge.

With a startled cry, the man in the Elvis mask stumbled backward.

❋ ❋ ❋

"Gummy!" I squawked, craning my neck toward her voice and struggling to untangle myself from the hysterical quintuplets inside the van. The quints flapped and shrieked and howled at the tops of their voices. The noise and confusion were incredible. I shoved my hands over my ears.

BANG!

Someone slammed a fist against the outside of the van. The quints sucked in one huge startled breath.

"Quiet!" Sid thundered. "Stop," he commanded. "Ma'am, stop."

"Get out of my way!" squalled Mrs. Gummidge. Her heavy footsteps padded up the driveway, and I heard her yelp, "Get your paws off me, you overbearing—"

"Oof," said Sid.

"I am *horrified,*" boomed Mrs. Gummidge, looming in the

doorway. "Let those children go. Immediately." The man in the Elvis mask tried to stop her, but she elbowed him in the stomach. She reached into the van and closed one big hand around Diane's arm and one around mine, preparing to haul us out of harm's way.

The man in the mask waved the gun angrily as if that might scare her away, but Gummy did not even see it. He bumped it against her shoulder, clicking his tongue impatiently. Gummy started to brush it away, then tightened her grip painfully, opened her eyes wide, formed her mouth around a silent "Oh" and froze.

"Stop right there," Sid ordered in a soft voice that sent a chill of terror through me. "Get into the van."

Mrs. Gummidge rolled her eyes toward him until the whites showed, only to find that he also had a gun pointed at her.

"I don't care what you do to me," she said in a small voice. "Just you leave these children alone."

Sid repeated, "Get in the van," and flicked the gun toward us.

Diane and I had to tug on Gummy's heavy arms to help her over the bumper, and when she settled herself down between us, she was wheezing from the effort.

"It's all wrong," I said. "I don't get this."

As if to prove my point, Sid turned slowly and pointed his gun at the man in the Elvis mask, who stared back at him uncomprehendingly through the eyeholes.

"You, too," said Sid. "Drop the gun. Get in the van."

"What?" said the man.

Beside me, Gummy stiffened and blinked. She stared at the Elvis man. Her hand tightened on my wrist.

"I said drop the gun," Sid repeated, and to our complete astonishment, the man did it. "Now, get in the van."

The man was backing up, shaking his head in a bewildered way, but Sid grabbed his arm and shoved him in beside us, slamming the door. The man did not fight. He slumped. He dropped to his hands and knees and whooshed out a dejected sigh that scared us and made us scoot away from him, tumbling over one another in the dim light.

Mrs. Gummidge let me go. She folded her arms across her chest. She seemed more disgusted than afraid.

Sid slammed the driver's side door, started the engine, and stepped on the gas. The van jerked forward, and the man in the mask crashed to the floor. There was a bump and thud of quints, who squealed and wriggled back against the wall.

"Awwww," groaned the man, grabbing at the mask as if he could no longer bear to be inside it. The rubber stretched alarmingly as he pulled at it. But after a second it popped from his head and he emerged pink-faced and sweating.

"Wilton Amaryllis," said Gummy in the semidarkness.

The quintuplets screeched.

"It weren't supposed to go like this," Wilton sobbed. He looked like a feverish child with his hair all sweaty and his eyes all scrunched up. He seemed ready to burst into tears. "Sid's a filthy traitor. It ain't fair."

The van swerved around a sharp corner. At any second we'd be moving up the side of the house, along the circular driveway. The guard at the gatehouse would not be the least bit suspicious of Sid. In fact, he would hurry to let the police van off the grounds, thinking Sid was busy with official business. I didn't know where he was taking us. I only knew I didn't want to go there.

I kicked the wall of the van and bellowed, "Help!"

"Help!" echoed the quints. We kicked and banged until the walls rumbled.

Wilton cursed a particularly black curse, slapped the rubber mask on the floor beside him, and dropped his head onto his knees. "He double-crossed me. That little ferret set me up! We were just going to leave the kids at her dad's place." He pointed toward me with his bottom lip. "Just for a kind of a . . . a gag, see? No harm done. I never would of done a real kidnapping. Just for a bit of a story, you know? A bit of cash."

Gummy was so mad she was practically spitting.

"You ridiculous little man," she raged. "I am outraged. What is the meaning of this?"

"Help!" we yelled, hammering the inside of the van until it thundered. "Let us out!"

Sid jerked the wheel left and then right to send us sprawling. Then he jumped on the brake. We crashed forward, hitting the wall so hard I lost my breath and two of the quints started crying.

Outside, something banged the roof of the van. Glass shattered. Quintuplets screamed, and Wilton Amaryllis gave a yell like an angry bear.

There was a crunch of metal and a brief ringing silence.

Chapter 27

My father had seen the kidnapping from the air. He did not know how to stop it, so he crashed the balloon—or, rather, the wicker basket of the balloon—right into us. He was up there, now, trying to gain control of the wildly swinging basket. I could hear propane roaring into the balloon. With a frantic mechanical buzz, the self-propelling device shifted into high gear.

But my father's heroics were not enough to stop Sid. The door flew open and he rushed toward us like an angry bear, dragging quintuplets over the bumper into sunshine, waving the gun. He was furious and terrified. I had never seen an adult who was so afraid. It stunned me.

A police car screeched to a halt, tearing a long muddy scar out of Wilton Amaryllis's lawn, but when the officers saw Sid, his gun, and the struggling quintuplets, they went into slow motion. They sank back into their car, terrified that he might shoot. They raised their hands and opened their eyes wide.

Sid glanced up at the out-of-control balloon. He was so scared he didn't care what happened. He fired into the sky.

The shot was so loud it was like being punched in the face. We froze, shocked by the sudden pain in our ears. It took long seconds to start breathing again. Everything rang.

Then he pointed the gun at me. I could see right into the round hole of the gun, and I could smell something sharp and hot. Gunpowder.

Nobody budged. The van's bumper pressed against the backs of my legs. Behind me, quintuplets sobbed.

When my father spoke, his voice was so close it made me jump.

"If you touch a hair on her head, I'll . . . I'll . . ." he yelled.

"Do *not* interfere!" shouted an officer.

But my father kept on. "Don't worry, Willie. Your dad's coming! Don't you *dare* hurt those children, you disgusting little . . . you measly little . . ."

Sid squinted up at him. It was a mistake. The looming balloon made him dizzy, and the sky dazzled him.

That's when my feet came up. I don't remember what I was thinking. I just balanced my weight on the bumper, took aim, and swung my legs as hard as I could. My left ankle cracked against gunmetal. With a crazy spinning motion, the weapon sailed away from us.

Sid fell forward onto his hands and knees.

❧ ❧ ❧

They didn't shoot him. Mrs. Gummidge said later that there were sharpshooters all around and that it would have been the work of an instant to put Sid into an early grave, but they didn't. They rushed forward like a wave, some officers moving heavily in their big boots, others looking like misplaced executives in their suits and sunglasses. Everyone was yelling.

"He was really going to kidnap them!" Wilton shouted. "Of all the . . . low-down dirty tricks!"

Sid was on his knees, struggling a little as someone fastened handcuffs on him. He grimaced. Then he looked up and aimed a cruel gaze at Wilton. A slow sarcastic smile crawled across Sid's face.

"You're strictly small-time," he said quietly. "I could have gotten a cool million for each of those kids. I could have been filthy stinking rich."

"You used me!" Wilton yelled. "We were supposed to be partners!"

Someone hauled Sid to his feet, and he dangled there like a schoolyard bully. Three officers held him while a fourth frisked him and a fifth told him, "You are under arrest."

For one brief moment before the crowd surged around him, he looked straight at me.

"You were going to kidnap us?" I asked numbly. "For money?"

He didn't reply. He just gave me the smile that used to dazzle me. It made me feel sick. I didn't even watch as they hurried him into the police car.

Mrs. Gummidge faced Wilton Amaryllis and began to yell.

"I *demand* an explanation!"

"He's a crook!" Wilton whined as they clicked the handcuffs behind his back. "I didn't mean no harm. He told me we were going to play, like, a little gag."

"A *gag,*" Gummy choked.

"You are under arrest," an officer told Wilton.

Wilton ignored him. "He said we were going to set up the crazy guy with the balloon. Make it look like *he* took the kids. You know. Get a story out of it."

"A story." Gummy's voice cut into him. He winced, but she went on. "A *newspaper* story." Wilton winced again. "To make money by selling a bunch of *lies.*" Gummy's breath came in fierce little gasps. "By terrorizing children. Is that what you call a *gag?*"

Wilton didn't reply.

"I guess those tabloids pay thousands for our family secrets," Gummy hissed. "So *that's* how you line your pockets these days?"

"I never would of hurt them kids," Wilton insisted. "That stinking Sid used me to get near 'em. He's a dirty double-crossing crook!"

And they hauled him away.

Chapter 28

No one reacted immediately to the sound of tearing fabric, the whoosh of angry flames, or the Tarzan yell of someone falling from a great height.

It was my father. There was a huge spruce tree on the far side of the lawn. He crashed the balloon straight into it. After his Tarzan holler, the balloon wrapped itself slowly around the tree, like someone too drunk to stand, and slid to the ground.

"Dad!"

My ankle hurt where I had smacked it against the gun, but I jumped up and ran as fast as I could. Arms stretched toward me and people shouted, but I dodged them. I headed toward the place where Dad had disappeared into a clump of bushes.

"It's on fire!" someone shouted.

The balloon had burst into a fountain of flame. Fire ran right up the bark of the spruce tree. A flap of rainbow-colored fabric collected clouds of smoke and spilled them up through the branches. The beautiful flying bubble disintegrated.

"Dad!" I yelled again, but suddenly my feet were running in midair. Someone lifted me right off the ground. For a dizzy moment I thought it was Sid, but of course it wasn't. It was Mr. Sweetwine.

"Come on!" A policewoman sprinted past us into the bushes. Two others followed her.

"Put me down!" I bellowed, kicking and twisting like a fish.

"Stop it!" said Mr. Sweetwine, tightening his grip.

I dangled above the driveway.

"Stop," he said again in a kinder voice. Behind him, someone's heels came clicking along the driveway, stumbling at first, then coming faster and faster.

"Willa!" My mother was hoarse. She grabbed me.

"Oh, God," she said. "Oh, God. Oh, my God."

"I'm all right," I said in a squashed voice.

"Oh, my God," she said again. "Are you sure? Are you absolutely sure?"

"Except you're squishing me," I said.

She did not seem to hear this. She stared over my head at the waves of heat and drifting smoke, where the remnants of the balloon lifted and settled in the branches of the spruce tree. Part of the banner—LOUISE!—streamed out like a flag, burst into flames, and vanished in a flash.

"There's your father," she said.

I whirled to see him emerging from the bushes, coughing and limping. He held one arm crookedly across his chest, and officers supported him from either side, but I could tell from the way he squinted toward me that he was all right.

"He's broken his arm," said my mother numbly, as she hurried across the lawn to meet him.

Mr. Sweetwine closed one hand on the back of my shirt to keep me from following, but I didn't even try. I was suddenly so tired I could have lowered myself onto Wilton's soft green lawn and curled up for a sleep. But I didn't. I just stood there with Mr. Sweetwine, watching my mother. She gestured and pointed toward me, giving my father a piece of her mind, hurrying along beside him, arguing.

My father didn't listen. He peered until he saw me, grinned, and waved his good arm. Emerging from the smoke, he seemed young and brave—a real hero. Then he tripped, and his glasses fell off, and everyone had to scramble around trying to pick them up again.

When I leaned against Mr. Sweetwine to wait for my parents, my laughter was coming in huge terrible sobs.

Chapter 29

A few days later, Gloria Fandango came back to finish the documentary.

"We got some breathtaking news coverage," she said, "and the barbecue was wonderful—if short—but we've still got to do these interviews. The whole documentary depends on them."

That's how I came to be sitting in the backyard with my five sisters around me. Gloria sat cross-legged on the ground, getting grass stains on her linen suit while my mother hovered nearby and pretended not to monitor everything we said. Fluffy purred in my lap.

For a second I forgot about the kidnapping. I glanced at the place where Sid used to appear when he was on patrol, and the old feeling of happy anticipation lifted up inside me. Then, with a crash, I remembered that Sid was in jail, and I remembered the gun and the kidnapping and his sarcastic smile, and I came back to reality with a thud.

"Tell me about your new sister," Gloria said. "When she first arrived, what did you think?"

Anne cleared her throat and sat up straighter. "Well," she said, "naturally we were very pleased about our father's wedding."

"Naturally," echoed Lianne.

"Naturally," Suzanne teased.

I couldn't help it. I burst out laughing.

Anne stammered. Then she giggled and confessed, "It was terrible." My mother looked up sharply, ready to intervene.

"What happened?" asked Gloria. "You seem to get along now."

The door of the servants' entrance swung open and my father came out. His arm was in a yellow sling.

"Well, for one thing, Willa kept saying she was going to live with her father," Marianne said.

The quintuplets laughed heartily as if this were a wonderful joke. I was glad my father was too far away to hear it, and I wished my mother was, too. Dad eased himself onto the doorstep, stretched out his legs, and raised his face to the sun.

Gloria persisted, "If you had a choice now, today, would you choose to be here with your mother or would you go back to your father?"

I did not know how to answer this. My mother was looking away from us, out over the river, listening.

"I don't know," I said at last. Gloria glanced over at my mother, who did not look at her.

"Do you still wish you could go and live with your father?" Gloria asked again.

The quintuplets watched me anxiously, waiting for my answer. As if they really wanted to know. As if it mattered.

"I don't know," I said again.

"Well, what about your father?" Gloria asked. "I suppose your mother's marriage to Prime Minister Sweetwine has made a big difference in your father's life?" Her bright news-hungry eyes drilled into me. The camera whirred on and on.

I gulped. It was Diane who answered for me, swooping in with a smile and a nod.

"Willa's father is wonderful," she said. "We like him *very* much. He is so imaginative and funny."

"Oh yes," Anne said. "Very funny. We all look forward to getting to know him better."

"Yes," Marianne agreed. "We like to think we have gained another parent. Don't we?"

Safe inside the chorus of quintuplet voices, I was free to study my father's dreaming expression. As he gazed out over the wide river, I knew he was remembering and regretting.

🍁 🍁 🍁

"Excuse me for a minute," I said and went to sit with my father. I linked my arm through his uninjured one and sighed.

Fluffy stood on her hind legs to rub her cheek on my hand. Her teeth grazed my knuckle. She was purring madly.

"The quintuplets are raving about you," I said, "on camera. You'll be famous."

He smiled sadly. "You're going to live here, with your mother, I guess," he said.

My throat closed up. The cat went suddenly out of focus.

"You don't need me at the shop." My voice wobbled. "You don't want me in your way all the time."

"Oh, certainly not," he teased, but his voice was sad.

I didn't say anything.

"Your mother," he said, "seems to feel that my big romantic gestures have been hurting you. Is that right?"

"No." I looked toward Gloria Fandango, who was laughing with the quintuplets. "Not exactly. It's just . . . well . . . when I first came here I thought your romantic gestures were really funny. But lately . . ."

"Lately, what?"

"Well. I mean, did you really think Mom would leave Mr. Sweetwine and go back to you?"

"Sure, she will. Eventually," he said. But I looked at him until he dropped his gaze and smiled uncomfortably. "I guess not," he said in a low voice.

"Because she won't," I said.

"I know. I knew that."

After a moment, he patted me on the knee. "Are you happy here, Willie?" he asked. "Happier than you are when you're with me?"

I swallowed hard. I couldn't say no. I couldn't say yes. The question made my thoughts go crashing into each other.

"The thing is, Willie," said my father, "I miss you."

If I spoke more than a couple of words, I knew my voice would dissolve, so I just said, "Me, too." My throat was so tight I didn't think I would ever swallow another thing.

I changed the subject. "This cat really likes you."

He stroked Fluffy, who chirruped contentedly.

"Mrs. Gummidge is furious because she has to look after her," I said, "while Wilton Amaryllis is in jail. You'd be doing her a big favor if you would take Fluffy back to Montreal with you."

"What would I do with a cat?"

"Feed her," I said. "Pet her. Keep her company. She's a national celebrity, you know."

He chuckled.

"Of course, you'll have to bring her here a lot," I said. "For visits. So she won't forget where she lives."

My father patted my hand and settled more comfortably on the step.

"I don't need an excuse to come visit you," he said.

That's where they got the footage for the closing credits of the documentary. You know the part I mean—where Dad kisses me on the forehead and Gloria Fandango talks about the importance of our ties to our parents. All of our parents.

That last little vignette is Mrs. Gummidge's favorite part. She likes that bit where the music fades away and the final credits hang in the center of the screen—the part where you can see her face at the kitchen door, calling, "Lunchtime! Wash hands, please!" and the sound track is suddenly full of the scrabble and rush of quintuplets leaping toward the house.

We must have watched it a dozen times on the TV in Gummy's sitting room. Every time we see it, she begins to whoop in a very un-Gummidgelike fashion, right when Fluffy spots the oncoming barrage of kids. The cat goes straight up in the air, I stumble sideways, and my father trips over the step. It isn't the domino effect of quintuplets that sets her off, Mrs. Gummidge says, or the sight of Gloria Fandango's grass-stained rump bobbing in and out of the picture.

"It's the thought of that absurd little Wilton Amaryllis," she says, mopping the tears of laughter from her cheeks, "watching this from his prison cell. Look what you've done to his rose bush! And look how you rumpled up his cat!"

Chapter 30

It was too quiet in my blue room. The sound of cars passing slowly down Sussex Drive was the loneliest sound I had ever heard. I dug through my closet for the *Happy Dooley* book and sat for a long time holding it on my lap.

Lucinda Dooley smiled up at me. I remembered how she felt when the gala ended, when she said goodnight to the famous movie star in his glittering mansion. I remembered how she became plain Lucinda Dooley again. I remembered how she got out of the limousine and ran up the path to the rented bungalow. She didn't feel sad. Her big happy family was waiting inside for her.

From across the hall, I heard a ripple of muffled quintuplet laughter, and it made my bedroom feel terribly empty. I tried to read a few pages, but the story kept slipping away. I kept stopping to listen to the silence of the big house.

Finally, I gave up. I collected my pillow, tucked the book under my arm, and padded down the hall to the quints' room. I stood there scrunching my toes in the deep carpet, trying to decide whether or not to knock. Inside, a quintuplet giggled.

I went in. The laughter stopped.

"Hi," said Marianne.

"Hi," I answered, steering through the beds and dressers, bathrobes and stuffed toys and board games to the empty neatly made bed under the window. I could see the moon out there, shining like a hot air balloon over the river.

"I've got a bedtime story for you," I said, plunking down my pillow and arranging a nest for myself in the lamplight.

I opened the old book, glanced nervously into the listening faces of the quintuplets, took a deep breath, and read, "When Lucinda Dooley was twelve years old, she chased a glittering dream of stardom all the way from Middleville, Illinois, to the bright lights of Hollywood. And everyone in her big happy family went with her."